AF191937

TRAUTE WOHLERS-SCHARF

NARCISSIST: QUO VADIS?

An extra-terrestrial visit at a
Turning Point of Time

The original text was written in
German and was translated by
the author

novum ◢ pro

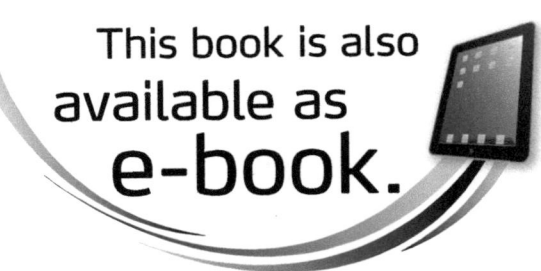

This book is also available as e-book.

www.novumpublishing.com

© 2023 novum publishing

ISBN 978-3-99146-373-3
Cover illustrations:
With friendly permission of:
Gallerie Nazionali di Arte Antica,
Roma (MiC) – Bibliotheca Hertziana,
Istituto Max Planck per la storia
dell'arte/Enrico Fontolan;
Teamarbeit I Dreamstime.com
Cover design, layout & typesetting:
novum publishing
Author's photo: Traute Wohlers-Scharf

www.novumpublishing.com

Climate neutral
Print product
ClimatePartner.com/16547-2201-1002

Contents

Preface 7

First Report
Status quo of aggression on the Blue Planet 11

Second Report
Hermetic principles in the field
of tensions in the narcissistic society 20

Third Report
Narcissist: Where are you from? 27

Fourth Report
The first Hermetic law – the Principle of Mentalism –
in the biography of Steven Hawking 37

Fifth Report
The second Hermetic law – the Principle of Resonance –
in the biography of Friedrich Schiller 43

Sixth Report
The third Hermetic law – the Principle of Vibration –
in the biography of Laotse 49

Seventh Report
Narcissism in the circle of family,
partnership and children 56

Eighth Report
The fourth Hermetic law – The Principle of Rhythm –
in the biography of Martha Graham 66

Ninth Report
Narcissism in the mirror of gender 71

Tenth Report
The fifth Hermetic law – the Principle of Polarity –
in the biography of Rainer Maria Rilke 80

Eleventh Report
The sixth Hermetic law –
the Principle of Cause and Effect –
in the biography of Agatha Christie 87

Twelfth Report
Narcissism and the Post-Growth Economy 94

Thirteenth Report
The seventh Hermetic Law – the Principle of Gender –
in the biography of Hildegard von Bingen 103

Homecoming to the Stars 111

General note 116

Preface

This book could not have been written in this form five years ago. And yet it contains nothing that could not have been thought and grasped for a long time ago.

To put it even more clearly: The facts described here were not only accessible to human thinking and feeling decades ago, but also in ancient times. What was missing, however, was the willingness, or even just the reason, to deal with the serious consequences of this development trend.

Aggression has always existed in interpersonal behavior. However, at present this has spread to a high percentage of mankind, predominantly in the western world. Additionally, the 'greed-economy' has become an accepted form on a collective level. On a personal level, people stick to the 'Do ut des' schema of 'I give so that you give'. This explains the inability to transcend the personal space and go from a 'having-consciousness' to a 'being-consciousness'.

In the recent past, a drastic surge of negative phenomena has taken place in many countries. A morbid society – with an octopus spread of power and information across national borders, to a worrying increase in aggressive violence, sexual abuse of children and young people, even bestiality – met a global pandemic in 2020-2022, and the aggressive war of Russia against Ukraine, starting on February 24th 2022.

The entire Blue Planet is in a state of upheaval. It is the beginning of an accelerated evolution. A turning point is announced. A similarly dangerous situation of a nuclear conflict already existed in the 1960s, when the democratic West, the USA and

Europe, faced the communist East, the USSR and its satellites. This crisis has been overcome.

Lotus, an alien visiting the Blue Planet, thinks in larger terms of time. He even includes Plato's legend about Atlantis in his considerations: A highly developed civilization, driven by pride – 'superbia' – had launched a war of aggression and attrition against countries of the Mediterranean, which finally led to a cataclysmic downfall 12.000 years ago.

Hermes Trismegistos, an Atlantean who later became the Egyptian Thoth – god of wisdom – imparted hermetic principles to other 'earthlings'. Only the inclusion of this wisdom and the hope for a change in the value system could counteract the current crisis.

This is the very mission of Lotus, who is investigating in the National Library in Vienna whether the qualities of 'earthlings', who acted and lived according to hermetic principles, could avert an atomic meltdown. Corresponding biographies are found for each of the seven hermetic laws – which are working throughout the whole cosmos and at all times:

1. Steven Hawking – the principle of the mind
2. Friedrich Schiller – the principle of resonance
3. Laotse and the Tao Te King – the principle of vibration
4. Martha Graham – the principle of rhythm
5. Rainer Maria Rilke – the Principle of Polarity
6. Agatha Christie – the principle of cause and effect
7. Hildegard von Bingen – the principle of gender

All of these people acted contrary to narcissistic behavior or solely for personal gain.

At the National Library, Lotus meets Marta, a young student who has just been dumped by her narcissistic friend and colleague. She has been dealing with the omnipresent topic of the narcissistic society already for a certain time. Now it has become her personal concern, which makes the analysis all the more emotional, but also more concise.

Driven by pain and disappointment, Marta, whose career goal is journalism, writes essays that characterize narcissism on a personal and collective level, (as well as the biographies of the three female representatives who lived according to hermetic principles):

- Myth and origin of narcissism
- Narcissism in the circle of family, partner and children
- Narcissism reflected in gender

Marta and Lotus see in narcissistic behavior an equally destructive danger within the western world as an external nuclear attack: narcissism as an internal atomic bomb with a collective danger of destruction.

The encounter and the subliminal intergalactic flirt between Lotus and Marta invites you to smile. But the results of the investigation of the very angry journalist about narcissism in family and partnership are explosive. This proves that the Blue Planet is threatened not only by an external nuclear bomb, but also by the internal danger of collective narcissism in interpersonal relationships.

Despite all the dangers of a doomsday scenario, it is also the blunt intention of this book to be entertaining. The visit and experiences of the alien Lotus on the Blue Planet are described as part of a sci-fi story – in the past one would have chosen the form of a fable.

Lotus is to take stock of the acute risk of nuclear annihilation of mankind. This would also upset the balance of galaxies when the Blue Planet becomes nuclear waste. The situation is hopeless but not serious, as they say in Austria. However, there is a meta-level that also displays positive solutions.

So the outcome of this sci-fi story is also optimistic and gives hope that the 'narcissus' flower can overcome the death of the beautiful youth Narcissus. The hermetic principles of Hermes Trismegistos – which so many special people followed in the past – may find many followers today.

This story aims to tell and convey knowledge from many eras, as well as to draw attention to dangerous behavioral symptoms that characterize contemporary society. The reader can turn to anywhere and start at any chapter. Where his interest is aroused, the bibliographical references should facilitate his access to the sources (which, however, only concern the Blue Planet and historical times).

The material compiled here is based on my more than 15 years of work as a psychotherapist (symbol drama), as well as my work as an economist in Africa (Senegal) and Asia (Philippines, Asian Development Bank), with many missions in countries on this continent, as well as in the OECD Development Center Paris. These experiences in different cultures have shown that human needs for acceptance and tolerance are the same everywhere, as are negative traits of life-threatening egocentrism.

At the end, a word of thanks should not be missing, to everyone who helped me with the writing of the book: Teachers, professors from many different faculties, colleagues, friends and many books shaped my understanding of the world and my writing style.

Dr. Renate Dorner carried out the first editing of the manuscript with commitment and care. Afrodita Posch was helpful in transferring the corrections, as well as suggestions for shortening and clarity. A big thank you to everyone.

Happy reading!

Status quo of aggression on the Blue Planet

Dear Gowinda!

Happily landed on the Blue Planet. Still quite dizzy, not only in the head, but in all limbs. Such a galactic beam is very exhausting.

Nevertheless, I immediately set to work, in the center of the chaos, in the point of absolute calm: the National Library in Vienna: a place with beautiful reading rooms, adorned with books from the walls to the ceiling. Few visitors, the holidays have begun.

It is a very special feeling to touch paper, to turn the pages, to smell these treasures. With us everything is digital, compressed into the smallest space, no personal contact. I know it, you are more pragmatic and see the advantages of the digital system. I felt a real nostalgia for the past when I finally received my first book order.

You guessed it right, it's the work of Konrad Lorenz: 'The so-called Evil. On the natural history of aggression.' I have finally been able to study this bestseller closely and can report to you amazing results.

This book was written exactly sixty years ago, with a note in the last chapters that the Blue Planet is observed from Mars. The father of the greylag goose Martina, as you now know, Konrad Lorenz, rightly remarked that an extra-terrestrial observer could not understand the reactions of terrestrial people in the course of history and the present, because they violate logos and common sense.

Two nations fight each other, even if no economic reasons compel them to do so. Two political parties or religions are relentlessly at war, despite the amazing similarity of their programs of salvation. The priests of the same religion of both conflicting parties bless the weapons.

An Alexander the Great and a Napoleon sacrifice millions of subjects in an attempt to bring the whole world under their sway. Curiously, the schools of the Blue Planet teach that 'earthlings' who have committed these and similar absurdities are to be worshiped as great men.

Sixty years ago, at the height of the Cold War, a possible escalation of a nuclear war between the two superpowers USA, the capitalist West and the USSR, the communist East, and their respective satellites, was dangerously high.

This dangerous cliff was successfully circumnavigated and a long period of peaceful coexistence followed, up until on February 24th 2022. There was an attack on Ukraine by Russia that trampled on all norms of international- and martial law. Together with other factors, such as the three-year global pandemic (which is still not over), climate change, energy crisis, inflation, danger of starvation in Africa and other third world countries, etc. – all these factors are leading to a Turning Point in history!

This development is not unknown to our Star and is also the reason for my mission: How bad is it on the Blue Planet? Is it still possible to avert the super catastrophe? Or is it already ten minutes past twelve?

At the time, Konrad Lorenz, a comparative behavioral scientist and Nobel Prize winner, described an analogy between animals and humans. As the magazine 'Der Spiegel' so aptly put it, Lorenz's conclusion 'from the goose to the whole' [von der Gans auf das Ganze] was and is controversial.

However, Lorenz's observations and conclusions of the animal world are noteworthy. His basic thesis is that aggression in animals and humans is a primal drive that has a species-preserving effect.

However, there is a fundamental difference between humans and animals: In the case of animals, all variants of aggression are never aimed at destroying their fellow animals, but at driving them away, or at placing them in a hierarchy, the pecking order. Thus aggression in animals is system- and lifesustaining, not destructive and a priori not 'evil'.

Aggression in animals is about attacking conspecifics, not about attacking prey, but about competition and rivalry for territory and females. In Darwinian terms, aggression is an instinct to preserve the species.

Carnivores are evolutionarily protected from destroying conspecifics by various mechanisms of inhibition of aggression. Man is not a predator. For a being only armed with weak teeth and short fingernails, there is no selective pressure to develop instinctive inhibitions against aggression. The invention of weapons changed the situation fundamentally. There was no time for opposing adjustment processes.

These martial items have spread rapidly. Even the hand axe is a global phenomenon. Man promptly used hand ax and fire to kill and roast his brother. This is proven by finds in the dwellings of the Beijing people: Next to the first traces of the use of fire there are smashed and roasted human bones.

However, the aggression, which can lead to murder and manslaughter, cannot be bred away. According to Lorenz, it would also be wrong to switch off this primal impulse, which is the driving force behind many human achievements in science and art, and has a species-preserving effect.

Lorenz gives three reasons for this, which apply to both humans and animals:

1. Through intraspecific aggression, the living space is divided up in such a way that each individual can make ends meet. The best feeding grounds/workplaces are defended against conspecifics who have to find their livelihood elsewhere.
2. The strongest/wealthiest males get the chance to produce offspring's.
3. The progeny is always aggressively protected in the animal world, mostly in humans, which also serves to preserve the species.

Lorenz also makes suggestions on how to compensate for the lack of balance between aggression and aggression inhibition in humans: redirection of the aggressive drive to substitute actions; ritualization of fights in sports and other competitions. This led to the smoking of the 'peace pipe' among the American indigenous people, which marked the end of any fighting.

Other important factors are education, science and art, which encourage mutual exchange and international friendships. Last but not least, humor has an aggression-inhibiting effect. He who laughs does not shoot. Dictators never laugh.

Lorenz also recognized that human beings are part of the overall context of nature and was ahead of his time. This also applies to his awareness of ecology. Unfortunately, also for his correct assessment that man's instinct for aggression cannot be compensated for by moral rules, as the current international political and economic situations show.

The nuclear threat of the superpowers is repeated today, and more than ever there is no inhibition of aggression. Russia's 'special operation' is not just a war of aggression, but a war of annihilation. After the enemy troops have withdrawn, no stone is left unturned, every life is wiped out. This type of aggression does not occur in the animal world.

Lorenz sees the contemporary human being as the link between the animal and the truly humane human being. It will still take a few development steps, and it will take some time for the Blue Planet dwellers to become real 'humane' beings!

To prevent humanity from mutually destroying and wiping out, we must intervene intergalactically. Nuclear waste on an entire planet upsets the cosmic balance!

Gowinda, I have to interrupt now, … A young lady is approaching me …

… Gowinda, I'm back. Something unlikely happened: I was exposed! But not seen through.

It was not a huge secret police man in a raincoat and dark glasses, but a mass of blond hair, a long tail, big blue eyes and a mouth that's always a little open in curiosity.

At that moment, I didn't know what betrayed me. I grabbed my tie, that choker that we no longer wear on our Star, which gives me the most unpleasant feeling of lack of air.

"Mr. colleague", it chirped, "a tie like that is really not necessary in this heat. Take a relief! Why don't you loosen up this stupid patricide. The ladies at the loan desk are already talking about you", I was told mockingly.

"But I wanted to ask you about something else," she continues inquisitively." You read so fast! You turn the pages so quickly and write on your smartphone at the same time. How do you do that? I've also taken speed reading classes, but it is astonishing the way you do it. And what model do you use? I have never seen that, and I follow every development in the digital system. "

Now I knew what betrayed me: my rapid reading. This young lady has no idea that I operate from the twelfth dimension, while she only has four dimensions at her disposal. I had to distract her now in this moment, although I had planned an adjustment period of at least one day to the terrestrial environment. So I discreetly cleared my throat and boldly jumped into the new language.

"I'm working on a sociological study of the rise in aggression in the last decade. And I have only a very limited time." I managed to choke out a little breathlessly, waiting for her reaction.

She was momentarily distracted by this almost truthful statement, especially by my 'galaxophone', which she had been eyeing longingly. And she enthusiastically began to talk about herself, as is also the case with females on our Star.

"I am a student after the first state examination, so I am 'cand. phil'. I haven't decided on my major yet. I hesitate between comparative literary studies, psychology and contemporary history. My career goal is to be a journalist. But you can't learn to write at university. Either you can do it, or you better leave it.

However, I have a minor question: You are doing a sociological study and reading Konrad Lorenz, who was mainly concerned with animals and his greylag goose Martina, right? Would you like to also consult 'Brem's Tierleben' and 'Maya the Bee' for human social life as well?"

I had to smile at the little rascal. But I also had to acknowledge that she had the right mindset for a future journalist.

"Oh that's great, you didn't snap at my funny remark. And you smile like Bruce Willis. You don't look much like him, but the smile has the same consistency: a mixture of benevolence and sarcasm. I like that a lot, so I'll take the liberty of commenting on your attire. Your suit is so crumpled, as if you had arrived from a second-class train, from Vorarlberg, directly in the National Library."

"I had come a little further than that. And the fabric was also exposed to extreme stress," I dared to defend my suit. My astronaut outfit paid little attention to my 'quasi underwear'.

"Oh, did you do martial arts? Or practice push-ups on your thumbs like Bruce Lee?" The imagination of the young lady knows no bounds. But now it was time to shift the discussion to my areas of interest. The best way to defend and distract is to attack.

"But why are you currently reading about the love live of French kings, when it isn't particularly related to your majors or minors?

"Oh, you can read over your head. And I was so sure that you didn't look at me and my reading. I'm trying to get some articles published, it's never too early to start.

Unfortunately, I haven't had any success so far. The press offices don't deny, they just don't get in touch for weeks and months. This is very frustrating. In doing so, I strive for topics that could at least make people smile in these dark times. Just listen: a French king wrote to his mistress after winning a battle: 'Madame, don't wash yourself anymore. I'm coming!'

Gowinda, I like this idea so much in its oddity and absurdity! What do you think about it?

Back to the would-be-journalist. I didn't just want to comfort her, I also wanted to open her new perspectives: "In Vienna, people are slow. Haven't you tried to place your articles internationally, for instance in Spanish speaking countries which include Latin America? You know what Gustav Mahler said: "If the end of the world is announced, then I'll go to Vienna. Everything happens there fifty years later."

"No, I hadn't thought of that", she said, amazed. "But I would also like to add that Vienna was almost the center of the world during the Austro-Hungarian monarchy. And that's not so long ago if you analyze history in sufficiently large periods.

A bodyguard from the former Yugoslavia said that his sister – several decades ago – felt disadvantaged among five brothers and also wanted a pee. When her mother remarked that it wasn't that easy, the girl answered firmly: "Why, you can buy anything in Vienna. That's where the center of the world is."

I gave in immediately and noticed that I was fully aware of the historical importance of the imperial-, capital- and residential city (Reichs-, Haupt- und Residenzstadt). Then I got back to Lorenz and his greylag goose Martina. "What do you think of the book about the so-called 'Evil' Isn't it outdated, is it still relevant?"

"How did you come up with this absurd idea? As far as aggression and lack of inhibition of aggression is concerned, Lorenz understated it. Unfortunately, that has long been proven sociologically and statistically. And this is true on both. personal and collective level. We can discuss it later.

I appreciate the old gentleman Lorenz with his greylag goose Martina, although he made a serious mistake in his book. He often quotes Goethe at the beginning of his chapters, but forgets 'Heidenröslein', which describes one of the most nasty forms of aggression: rape! These verses belong to the love poems of world literature, although the word 'love' does not appear once in it."

She notices from my questioning look that I'm not particularly well versed in the poetry of the Blue Planet. But my charming colleague wants to enlighten me and starts to quote.

"If a boy saw a little rose, little rose on the heath,"(Sah' ein Knab' ein Röslein stehn, Röslein auf der Heiden) … At the beginning a young man discovers a little rose on the heath, whereby the rose is to be understood as a girl. This girl is young and very beautiful and the boy fell in love with her immediately. He is in a love frenzy. The first verse has an euphoric and longing mood. In the second stanza the boy wants to pick the little rose, whereupon the rose threatens him.

"I'll break you" the boy, "I'll stab you", the girl. If a rose is broken off, it loses its life energy supply and will die. The rose then has to 'suffer'. In this stanza the basic mood has changed from euphoria to a tense conflict. In the third and last stanza, the boy commits the announced act of violence and breaks the little rose. The boy is described as wild, he is not impressed by the pricking of the rose.

Even moaning doesn't help the little rose, the girl doesn't manage to defend herself and 'just has to suffer', nature takes its course. The boy wants to make the beautiful his own, grasp it and experience it. This desire is stronger than any suffering that he inflicts on another human being. This is the way every narcissist acts."

Then the lady-student continues to relate the poem to the present. "Goethe wrote this poem in 1770 and it seems that until the 21st century such an offense was not punished by the judiciary, not even as a minor offence.

But recently there has been a bang finally. A royal coffer had to fork out tens of millions of pound to save a prince from a civil lawsuit for having sexual relations with a minor girl. The criminal court is still pending. There was probably a negative 'prince discount'. But such an event has a global impact when such offenses are finally punished as crimes."

A red face looks at me defiantly.

"But why wasn't this omission of Goethe's poem, in this particular context, remarked earlier?" I inquired.

"Because all famous literary critics are men. And they have many blind spots and see many things very differently. Hasn't it struck you that women and men are as different as if they belong to two different species of animals?"

18

But here I had to protest. After all, it is very difficult for different animal species to breed together.

"Reproduction is not the only criterion that counts. It depends on the way of thinking. Mind is above matter!"

And now I definitely wanted to get a real dialogue going. The blond student had postulated the first hermetic principle – almost only as a subordinate clause – while the whole adult world on the Blue Planet is only chasing after material goods.

"May I introduce myself, my name is Lotus," I said rising and bowed as I had read in the guides to etiquette of this planet – der Knigge.

"And I'm Marta, very pleased. But sometimes it seems to me that you come from the moon."

"Oh no, a little further" I remarked cockily.

"Stop these stupid jokes. Now I'll give you a valuable advice: Go to Mariahilfer Strasse, get blue jeans and several T-shirts, preferably with Dracula, dragons or similar creatures on the hero's chest.

You have to stand out in order not to stand out. You don't want to attract attention and you do everything wrong. But I like you, sir. See you tomorrow. Then we talk about speed reading and ..."

"... the smartphone," I added. She smiled happily and was gone.

Lorenz had his greylag goose Martina, and the duckling Marta has me. She shaped me, and I will duck-step her to complete this mission successfully and soon.

Gowinda, I embrace you from a galactic distance, but nevertheless, deeply!

With love,
Lotus

First alpha-mail to Star Omicron 007
Sent and received!

Hermetic principles in the field of tensions in the narcissistic society

Carissima Gowinda!

I had a wonderful 'Margherita' in a pizzeria in the national colors of Italy. And the cook sang 'la donna e mobile'. If it weren't so far away, beyond the Milky Way, I would suggest a pleasure trip together to the land of the 'bel canto'!

This 'joie de vivre' is in stark contrast to Central European countries, especially Austrian misery feelings. Pretty much everything here is difficult, complicated ... and inefficient. The Viennese are so fond of grumbling, and the ladies at the book loan desk refuse to accept more than a very limited number of orders. They have no idea how fast I can read. People here find a problem for every solution.

No wonder, the hermetic principles have not fallen on fertile ground on the Blue Planet. However these cosmic laws can be found in many sacred scriptures, in vedic texts, the Bible, in the holy books of the Persians. The majority of people today hardly follow them at all.

Four thousand years ago, a wise man from the continent Atlantis, Hermes Trismegistos had tried to teach hermetic principles to other 'earthlings'. He was a philosopher and priest, in Egypt he became Thot: the god of the moon and wisdom.

This mission was then called 'galactic colonization'. But not in the sense of terrestrial colonization: There it means simply exploitation of people and resources. We understand this concept as enabling a whole planet to make a leap in consciousness. And such a process enriches the whole universe, if it succeeds!

Hermes Trismegistos, the Threefold Sage, formulated these cosmic principles for earthlings and recorded them on emerald tablets. They were later passed on orally under the name 'Kybalion'.

It was a great gift: It is a structure of laws according to which the universe, the entire cosmos, is working. They are laws of consciousness that affect people mentally and emotionally. They work throughout the universe and are always active. The law of gravity, for example, only works in the Earth's atmosphere. That is why the astronauts float in space capsules when they have reached the stratos- and mesosphere.

The Hermetic laws are a model that shows connections between one's own life and that of other people. If you are aware of these laws, you can determine the direction of your life, your career, your life partners. The dependence on external events and influences is thus significantly reduced. One would think that these would be desirable goals, but very few people care about them on the Blue Planet.

It was not until 1908 that these laws became known to the general public in the United States with the publication of Kybalion. The authors of this work are unknown, 'Three Initiates' published the book.

The meaning of Kybalion is unclear. It could have to do with cybernetics. Literally translated it means 'ship captain'. It could express that sometimes people need help and support to get through difficult situations. "Anyone who travels without a guide takes two hundred years for a two-day trip", says a Chinese proverb.

The seven Hermetic Principles are briefly presented below. And then I will look for biographies of people who acted and lived according to these laws. All these earthlings have achieved extraordinary feats and have been an enrichment for all humanity.

The cosmic principles sound very theoretical at first, but there are concrete ways of applying them in everyday life, if you reflect on them.

1. The Principle of Mentalism and Creation: "All is spirit, the universe is spiritual," quotes the Kybalion.
   The origin of life is mental. Thoughts initiate change and create something new. The universe is infinite and humans are just a part of it. Therefore, their perceptions are also limited, because a part can never understand the whole.

2. The Principle of Resonance: "As Above, so Below. As Within, so Without, and as in Large, so in Small". Kybalion
   This Law of Resonance is based on the idea that like attracts each other, while unlike repels each other. This also has an effect in literature, at a certain point in time, when a topic becomes relevant to everyone on the globe, it has an echo in the hearts of all beings.

3. The Principle of Vibration: "Nothing is still, everything moves, everything vibrates." Kybalion
   Standstill does not exist. Even things that appear immobile vibrate at the atomic level. The whole universe is built like this, big and small. The planets revolve around the sun, and the smallest particles, ions and electrons, revolve around each other. Everything is permeated with vibrations, so everything is connected.

4. The Principle of Polarity: "Everything is twofold, everything has its pair of opposites. Equal and unequal are the same. Opposites are identical in nature, only different in degree. Extremes touch; all truths are only half-truths." Kybalion
   There is no such thing as good or bad, it is the perspective that counts. Where there is light, there is also shadow. High and low, small and large, always form two opposite poles that cannot exist without each other. This also applies to life and death.

5. The Principle of Rhythm: "Everything flows in and out, everything has its tides, all things rise and fall. The swing of

the pendulum shows in everything, the amount of swing to the right is the amount of swing to the left. Rhythm compensates." Kybalion

This concept means that everything is impermanent. Neither happiness nor sadness lasts forever. The center of gravity constantly swings from one pole to the other. This creates a cycle that determines life: On a small scale, like breathing, and on a large scale, like in the plan of life and destiny.

6. The Principle of Cause and Effect: "Every cause has its effect. Every effect has its cause, everything happens according to law. Coincidence is but the name of an unknown law." Kybalion.
Every action is followed by a reaction. Nothing happens without a reason. God does not play dice. This principle is included in the other Hermetic laws. This principle always works and forms the basis for the other laws.

7. The Principle of Gender: "Gender is in everything, everything has male and female principles, gender is revealed on all levels." Kybalion
Everything has male and female parts. Gender is always revealed, not only on the physical but also on the mental plane. There is no one and nothing in the universe that is fatherless or motherless. Every idea needs space to materialize, just like the seed needs time to mature and grow. There are special people who combine these two aspects in harmony.

So much for the description and definition of the Hermetic Principles. And now comes an analysis of the contemporary narcissistic society in which these laws should be applied if the Blue Planet is to survive.

Many historians and sociologists speak of a rapid increase in narcissism in the recent past and the present. Numerous scientific studies point to a permanent increase in the basic elements of narcissism: self-infatuation, egocentricity, self-ag-grandizement, ruthlessness, lack of empathy, extreme sensitivity to criticism, etc.

The reason for the ever increasing self-focus is probably a change in the canon of values towards self-confidence, realization of one's own ego, self-portrayal while putting aside values such as solidarity, integrity, responsibility, etc.

According to numerous studies, the increased self-centeredness, both on a personal and collective level, has reached a destructive extent so that any sense of community has largely disappeared. A list of reasons for this development is given, enabling circumstances, psychosocial preparedness and increased vulnerability, also play a role.

Changing moral concepts and values are important factors. Former virtues such as modesty, frugality and subordination are now seen as more of a blemish and are viewed as old-fashion. One's own needs are placed even more at the center of interest than in the times of the Renaissance. The new ideals are self-confidence, consumption, control and self-reference.

The dominant effect of the present has become 'being cool'. Anything that gives pleasure, that is successful, that satisfies is cool. Hard-nosedness, lack of excitement and lack of sensibility play an important role. These are all narcissistic elements. A connection between the new orientation of the emotional world and an unempathetic-narcissistic attitude is obvious.

Constant stress, hectic pace and increased professional requirements leave no room for empathy, consideration, understanding or clarifying discussions in this elbow society. The modern earthling has to assert himself, reach his goal directly and at the same time remaining accessible – and therefore – remaining disruptable.

Another development to narcissism is the power of information that is now available. What could better convey the feeling of omnipotence than being able to receive any information at any time and in any place? This 'click sovereignty' conveys a narcissistic elation. Boundless communication has become a matter of course for IT-people. This promotes the feeling of uniqueness, superiority and power – in short, narcissism.

There have been many technical, medical and social developments that have made work and life easier for the Blue Planet inhabitants. The sweat on the face is hardly a prerequisite for earning a living. The longing for the golden age, in which the work of machines replaces that of humans, has long since been fulfilled.

As far as the Western World is concern, Planet Earth is no longer a vale of tears. Life has become less a yoke than a pleasure. Power relations that made people unfree, bondage and hopelessness no longer exist in western civilization. Thanks to the development of medicine, especially the eradication of epidemics such as plague and cholera, both life expectancy and quality of life have increased significantly.

The Earth dweller has changed from a begging recipient to a courted consumer. In the past, there were frequent famines. But who has eaten his bread with tears, who has starved involuntarily? The modern man has to deal with excess and go to a fitness center to stay, or get in shape.

The modern citizen has many reasons to feel unique in historical comparison. But there have always been narcissistic people. The only question that arises is why there is a constant 'ego inflation' taking place in the Western World right now.

Social ties within family and community have been weakened by recent technological and economic developments. The self-representation of a self-loving society rushed into this vacuum. An obsessive desire to always be the center of attention emerged.

Self-actualization has set in motion a momentum of its own that can hardly be controlled any longer: Intensified capitalism, belief in achievement and growth, ruthless pursuit of profit and greed are expressions of a narcissistically disturbed society.

People have become more demanding, ruthless and selfish. The feeling of one's own grandiosity, self-idealization and devaluation of others seems to have developed into a modern principle of life.

The 'Zeitgeist' is increasingly determined by arrogance, lust for glory and macho posturing. This new 'socialization type' not only shapes the personality and self-esteem of the individual, but also has a significant social effect. The addicted desire for recognition desolidates society, undermines the community and isolates the individual. Narcissism has always existed in all societies. However, this was reserved for the rulers and the upper classes. In Europe this was the aristocracy and the clergy. But today, acting out the narcissistic needs, inherent in all human beings, has become a mass phenomenon.

Recent technological and economic developments allow a much larger percentage of the population to act out their narcissistic tendencies and realize narcissistic aspirations. What is new about society's narcissism is not its occurrence, but that it is sought as a way of life. This basic social attitude determines the 'Zeitgeist' – and heralds a Turning Point in history.

Gowinda, I hope that my stocktaking of the situation of the Blue Planet is not too gloomy, that the crisis cannot be overcome with our intergalactic help.

With affection,
  Lotus

Second alpha-mail to Star Omicron 007
  Sent and received

Narcissist: Where are you from?

My dearest Gowinda!

Now your Latino-American language skills are required. I didn't store translation programs on my 'galaxo-phone' because I couldn't imagine needing them. Reality is always more imaginative than our expectations. This story is long, I will tell it to you briefly.

Today I had already worked a few hours in the National Library. Marta's seat stayed empty, and I assumed she was taking a day off. That wasn't the case. Just before noon, someone approached me with a shy smile.

"I invite you to coffee and biscuits in the canteen. Do you have time, please?" It was Marta, and I almost didn't recognize her. The blond shock of hair hung down sadly, her nose and eyes were quite red, and her whole figure expressed sorrow and heartache.

I was deeply troubled by the sudden change from a fun-loving student to a sad creature of misery. I suspected a death in the family and waited for Marta's story.

The coffee with whipped cream, called 'Einspänner', did her good and she unpacked biscuits. "According to a recipe from Hildegard von Bingen, who lived in the twelfth century," she explained. "These are energy cookies with spelt, grated almonds, nutmeg, cloves and honey."

Marta wasn't yet ready to talk about her pain. So I tried a little joke and noticed that these biscuits also had a rather medieval shape: They were at least two centimeters thick and had a rather dark baking color.

"I know the cookies stayed five minutes too long in the oven, but they still taste good and they really give me energy. I need this now.

By the way, I like your T-Shirt with the smiling dragon. We need a name for the animal: how about Filofax?"

"Agreed Marta. I've bought Filofaxes in all the colors of the rainbow. That was my weekly plan."

"You only plan for such a short time, that is not very efficient. I always plan in much longer periods of time," she said with great determination.

"Hasn't one of your plans already gone sour lately?" I wanted to help Marta to finally address what had caused her so much pain. "Isn't there a saying: If you want to make God smile, then plan." Then I added: "If there are too many unknowns variables, then planning becomes pointless."

"I don't agree with that," came the belligerent reply. "Sometimes decisions have to be made ad hoc, even when there are still many unknowns in the equation.

Just think of Julius Caesar, when he crossed the river Rubicon with his army – and thus broke the law that no general was allowed to approach Rome with his army. He didn't say: 'The die is cast', as the philistines quote. He said: 'The dices are thrown up!' Victory and defeat were still undecided. But Caesar dared."

"Marta, it doesn't have to be always so dramatic. What happened that you want to tell me? Maybe I can help."

Two deeply sad eyes blinked at me between tears. This is how the end of the world will be announced, I thought with trepidation. And then Marta burst out:

"I let myself be cheated and lied to. HE went on vacation without me! And then he left a sleazy letter saying I was to blame for his failure on the university exam because my notes weren't complete. I only write down what I don't know yet. I just leave out the familiar. And then another biting remark about my unpublished articles, which allegedly made any vacation planning impossible. At the end there is a sentence like … 'mille choses' …!

I couldn't imagine something like this happening. At the beginning of the semester everything was so wonderful. I felt understood like never before. Not only was he friendly, he always knew exactly what I wanted, what little things made me happy. He manipulated me in such a way that I didn't recognize this as a strategy. Narcissists have two faces: One side of this nasty game is called 'love bombing'.

Yesterday I got to know the other side: 'disposed of', because I'm no longer useful ad hoc! Above all, I get angry and hurt with myself. His charming promises have never been followed by actions. That should have warned me that sweet remarks were just a manipulative maneuver."

Now her mood changed radically and she got really angry: "Although there are no statistics on this, I estimate that at least three victims are exploited and humiliated by every malignant narcissist. You can't leave it like that. Something has to be done about it. At first I was so frozen yesterday that I couldn't eat, drink or sleep. But then an 'anti-narcissistic rage' seized me, which made me very active: I grabbed the pen, that's my sword.

Not to help the narcissists out of their entanglement, they don't want to change. That's what almost all relevant therapists say. Actual and potential victims must be informed and warned. It is unbelievable that some people live in such a toxic relationship for years, sometimes even decades! I will build my journalism career on narcissistic abuse because my 'anti-narcissistic anger' knows no bounds!"

And then she broke off, sobbing overcoming her. I was stunned by the – in my opinion – harmlessness of her situation. But I knew Marta had to see that for herself. Now she wasn't ready yet. She didn't need advice on the ridiculousness of the malicious letter, she needed to pour out her heartache.

A narcissist had exposed himself. He had the classic parameters of the disorder: Constant blaming of others for his own failures; envy of possible successes of his partner, devaluation of other people, lack of empathy, cold feelings, deceit: it was agreed to go on vacation together. Marta had fallen in love with a narcissist and blindly trusted his feelings – because she wanted to trust.

She should be glad to be rid of such a stupid bully. But you have to work out this knowledge yourself. According to a famous book, a classic, 'Men are different. Women too', by John Gray (1992), the females of planet Earth are from Venus, and the males are from Mars. So their basic needs are very different. Any logical argument in such a situation is pointless.

"Marta, may I invite you for a hot chocolate? Then we will eat Hildegard's energy biscuits with a delicacy that this clever abbess didn't even know: cocoa! That was the secret of the red Indians."

"Agreed. please order. I wanted to use one of your recommendations: You suggested that I try to publish my articles in other languages, for example in Spanish.

My first foreign language is French. I'm not that familiar with the language of Garcia Lorca. Could you please translate my series of articles on narcissism? I'll pay you too, ten percent of my fee, or even more." Marta looked at me questioningly, and I just nodded in surprise at the new turn of the conversation.

"You may also be interested in my new ideas: I want to write a series of articles about narcissists in all variations, to warn everybody. All narcissists operate according to the same patterns, it's always the same scam. They are easy to see through once you know their strategies. I finished the first post last night and this morning.

Theoretically, I've been dealing already with this ubiquitous topic for a long time. But now it has become a personal issue. Here's the first draft". And she slid a stack of paper together with an USB stick across the table.

Marta has cognitively grasped the situation with her former boyfriend correctly, even though her heart is still bleeding a lot. I would like so much to help her to a journalistic success. In addition, her reflections and personal experiences are not uninteresting for the general analysis of the Blue Planet.

Therefore I ask you, Gowinda, for a translation and, if necessary, small corrections. But please in the fourth dimension, otherwise Marta's warlike outpourings will not be printed, because the twelfth dimension of our star Omicron 007 is incomprehensible to the 'earthlings'. Now I am sending you her first article as an attachment.

With many terrestrial greetings and kisses.
    Forever, your Lotus!

Marta's article:
'Narcissist, where are you from?' A victim's voice.
Today we live in a society that has become increasingly selfish. Some people are specialists in exploiting, deceiving and belittling all beings that come in touch with them. They lie so persistently that they could even outwit lie detectors. Their heart rate or breathing rate will not increase with such mundane activities as lying.

And there are more and more who perceive this lifestyle as 'cool'. Basically, they behave like vampires, covering their inner emptiness with the attention and feelings of their caregivers.

I fell into such a trap myself, although my gut feeling had been warning me for a long time. If only I had read professor H. Haller's book 'The Narcissism Trap' (2013), more closely. His lectures are also so clear and empathetic with the victims. However, the heart knows reasons that the mind can and will not understand. But once the brain has grasped the backgrounds and motifs, such a great misfortune and pain can no longer happen.

Thank you to all the narcissists that I have come across, in quite large numbers lately. I want my journalism career to be built on their dunghills. They inspired me to create this series of catalogs of narcissism and its manifestations to, if not put a stop to, at least limit their influence. Just as the ancient Romans put 'cave canem', (caution, biting dog) in front of their entrances, so I announce: 'Caution, narcissists!'

We have reached a Turning Point in history, we no longer have time for years of therapy with criticism-resistant patients who don't want to change at all. If at all, they only come to therapy, if they are forced to. In a situation where war is declared and nobody goes, war cannot take place. When empaths don't play the narcissist's game, there can be no more narcissistic exploitation.

If we don't play along with the narcissist's manipulations and feints, they will lose their game. They need admiration and praise like a fish needs water. When we withdraw, fully aware of the consequences of our actions, we have presented the narcissist with an existential choice: Change or end the relationship.

The narcissist would never have believed his partner capable of this action and makes him lose the ground under his feet. You have to be willing to live with the consequences and not be afraid of them. But better an end with misery, than misery without end. A narcissist senses and recognizes exactly whether his partner is serious about this threat.

Now back to the beginning. If one wants to understand the current social phenomena of narcissism, a return to the myth of Narcissus is essential. In this story, the ancient Greeks painted a deep-psychological picture that contains ancient wisdom, timeless knowledge of human nature and anticipates psychoanalytic thoughts.

The tale of the beautiful young man in love with his own reflection is a timeless myth. We owe the best-known literary tradition to the Metamorphoses of the Roman writer Ovid.

Narcissus is the son of the nymph Leiriope and the river god Cephissus. He had drawn this beautiful creature into his wake and did violence to the nymph caught in the waves. After that he flowed on unconcernedly, leaving the pregnant woman alone. Vulgo: He discarded her.

Leiriope gave birth to a beautiful boy whom she named Narcissus. The worried mother turned even to the seer Teresias to ask him if the lovely child would have a long life. The fateful spell was: "Until he knows himself."

Leiriope could not do anything with this prophecy, and was all the more concerned. Narcissus grew into a charming youth and was swarmed by girls and boys; even gods found favor with him. But he was untouchable, cold and hard-hearted.

The nymph Echo, who was cursed by Juno to only be able to repeat sentences because she had covered Jupiter's love games with beautiful nymphs, had fallen particularly in love with him. When Echo confessed her love to Narcissus, he rejected her with the words: "I want to die before I belong to you!".

The one so despised hid in the forest, took no more food, and finally passed away. Only her voice – the echo – remained. After disappointing many other suitors, Narcissus was cursed: "It will be the same for you, you shall never have what you love."

'Rhamnusia', the nemesis worshiped in Rhamnous, heard this curse and granted this request. One day, after a hunt, Narcissus wanted to quench his thirst at a clear spring. As he bent over the water, he saw a beautiful young man in it. He was mesmerized and couldn't get enough of the sight. He fell in love with the image he saw and was seized with consuming longing.

Lying on the floor, he tried to approach the beloved face. He couldn't. In agony he screamed out his pain, his unfulfilled love. Full of longing he bent lower and lower over the source. He came close to the image, but never reached it. Desperately trying to reunite with the beloved face, he fell into the flood and drowned.

Condemned to immortal self-love by the goddess of vengeance, haughty Narcissus, who pushed his beauty to arrogance, fell in love with his own reflection, discovered in the water of a pond. Nobody was found at the site of his death, but a flower: the daffodil – 'Narzisse. The transformation into a flower no longer came from Ovid's pen, but is one of the many variants of the story of Narcissus.

One of the best-known and most evocative depictions of this myth comes from Michelangelo Merisi da Caravaggio, an Italian Baroque master who created the painting between the years 1597 and1599. The picture impresses with strong light-dark contrasts, which enhances the intimacy of the scene, making it almost meditative. Narcissus' eyes are deeply shaded, his lips are luscious, and his longing gaze is fixed on black water.

Caravaggio conveys a dark melancholy in this painting, so that this water can be associated with the water of the Styx, with death. This painter led an eventful life in Rome, was often involved in fights and he was a killer. The subject of death was not unknown to him.

The brief narrative of the myth contains a wealth of psychological facts and hypotheses. The relationship problems between the parents, violent procreation, the broken-home situation are addressed. Add to that the overprotectiveness of a single mother. Such a situation can also be the case when the father is physically present, but emotionally absent.

The ancient wisdom warns against the addictive nature of selfishness. The final stretch of any addiction, including egoism, ends in loneliness, isolation, depression and often suicide, or even extended suicide, taking close family members, also children, with them.

The myth shows pathological developments and offers timelessly valid descriptions of a disturbed personality structure. Narcissism occurs in all social classes, often just in the best circles.

The violence used in conception may not have been physical in nature, but an emotional pressure, an entanglement. The 'flow around' could mean charming courtship. False promises, alcohol, drugs, or even K. O. drops may have been used. A narcissist has no remorse or inhibitions. Narcissus' biological father moved on after he was satisfied, he did not take note of the pregnancy, or simply forgot about it.

Has the missing father figure negatively influenced the child's development, perhaps in relation to reality and the ability to relate to other people? Did the father's lack of corrective structure encourage a tendency to daydream? The child Narcissus was spoiled and admired by the overwhelmed mother.

The myth also addresses the dangers of a spoiled upbringing. This causes the child to have a low tolerance for frustration and an excessive sense of entitlement. The feelings that are shown to the beautiful young man cannot be returned. He is incapable of love, emotionally illiterate.

At the same time, Narcissus is incapable of relationship, he is incapable to form an emotional bond with other persons.

Emotional coolness, detachment, preference for solitary occupations, such as hours of computer games, fantastic ideas about himself, his talents and his future are his characteristic parameters.

His caring mother even went to a 'seer' to prevent any danger. Prophecies are always vague and uncertain. They are often not understood at all. The oracle says, it's often better, if you don't know everything about yourself. This probably points to the dangers of looking at the shadow, the abysses of the soul, the evil in people. A radical psychoanalysis, which defoliates and relentlessly reveals repressions, as well as family constellations in large groups have already led to suicides.

Furthermore, the story of Narcissus tells that he surrounds himself with yes-people, those who submit and have no opinion of their own. That is what the nymph Echo, which only repeats everything, stands for. These are his favorite reference persons who admire him uncritically.

The fateful look in the mirror of the spring water brings knowledge, but not in a positive way. Narcissus sees what he has always been looking for in the illusionary image, which triggers an unprecedented feeling in him.

Now he could finally love. At last this unknown emotion could be felt. However, Narcissus did not fall in love with a person, but with an image. He is deeply touched, fascinated and caught by his reflection. Falling under an illusion, he falls himself.

The story of Narcissus is timeless. This problem is a basic human condition. Self-aggrandizement, extreme vulnerability, lack of empathy, inability to relate, existed even before the myth came into being. And the phenomena of narcissism will always accompany humanity. It is a basic problem of human existence, but it has to be kept in certain limits.

However, in the present, narcissistic attitudes seem to have become all the rage, gripping and shaping society in its entirety to an unprecedented degree.

'I, more I, most I', is the life principle of the narcissist. Because ego is paramount, selfishness is the opposite of altruism and community. Old-fashioned virtues of humanity, caring, responsibility are only laughed at. Feelings and needs of other people are simply ignored by the 'I'. In psychology, egoism is seen as an infantile attitude caused by a lack of development in the child's brain, which is not mature enough to make right and good decisions.

So the egoist builds an invisible wall around himself. He is everything, the world is nothing. Or, he is the world. And so there is not only the danger of an atomic bomb from external enemies, but unfortunately also an internal atomic bomb in Western society that is just as destructive: Narcissism. The narcissist first destroys those he relates to, and then he himself becomes a victim of his addiction.

He acts like the famous scorpion being carried across water by a frog. In the middle of the river the scorpion stings the frog. The dying animal asks, "Why are you killing me? You'll die in the floods too." The answer: "I can't help it. I'm a Scorpion, that's my nature!"

To be continued ... Martha ...

Post scriptum by Lotus: But I have to counter this gloomy analysis by Marta with another option for the Blue Planet. Marta herself mentioned that at the place of the dead Narcissus, at the edge of the spring, a flower opened. It stands for rebirth and the power to overcome darkness, evil and even death!

There is not only one variant of the myth with a happy ending, the universe offers other rescue options: There have always been people who acted and lived according to the Hermetic laws. I will compile these biographies and send them to you, as the basis for the final report on the dangerous and explosive situation on the Blue Planet.

The first Hermetic law – the Principle of Mentalism – in the biography of Steven Hawking

"The very softest in the universe penetrates through the very hardest, the invisible penetrates through the visible." – Tao Te King

There is probably no person in the present and recent past who has represented the Principle of Mentalism and Creation as well as Steven William Hawking. He lived in England from 1942 to 2018 and was a brilliant astrophysicist. S.W. Hawking provided important work on cosmology, general relativity theory and black holes. (A black hole is a region of space/time from which nothing, not even light, can escape due to its strong gravity.)

Steven Hawking made these brilliant discoveries despite being diagnosed with a degenerative motor nervous system disease, amyotrophic lateral sclerosis (ALS) in 1963, when he was just twenty-one years old.

At that time, doctors predicted that he would only live a few years. Despite this terrible diagnosis, he continued his studies at Cambridge University and pursued an academic career. From 1979 to 2009 he was 'Lucasian Professor of Mathematics', a chair held by Isaac Newton in the second half of the 17th century.

Steven Hawking had been confined to a wheelchair since 1968. In 1985, he lost the ability to speak due to severe pneumonia. Since then he has been using a speech computer for verbal communication.

And this personality formulated the following quote: "Even if I cannot move and I have to speak through a computer, in my head I am free!"

For many people, with a physical affliction or even an allergy – which can severely impair the quality of life – this is an encouragement, not to focus on the defect but on the creative power, unbroken by the physical affliction. The origin of life is mental in nature. And spirit always rules over matter. The whole life of S.W. Hawking, his very existence, is a testament to this Hermetic Principle.

Through his popular scientific books on modern physics and extensive media coverage, he also became known to a wide audience outside of the scientific world. His theories are based on the idea that all that exists is permeated by an intelligent spirit. This also explains that everything is connected. Everything influences each other, even if you cannot consciously perceive these influences.

His dissertation 'Properties of expanding universes' is a topic that occupied him long after his doctorate. The boundary condition of the universe is that it has no boundary. This is a natural formulation for problems of quantum cosmology. There are probably still a few unanswered questions in this regard.

Hawking's first popular science book, 'A Brief History of Time', was published in 1988. In this work he presents the theories of the origin of the universe, quantum mechanics and black holes. The book became a bestseller worldwide and sold millions of copies.

It stayed on the Sunday Times bestseller list for 237 weeks, longer than any other book (excluding the Bible and Shakespeare). It has been translated into about forty languages. "My books on physics sell better than Madonna's books on sex," the author proudly remarked. (I wonder if all buyers have studied the book to the end?)

The success of 'The Brief History of Time' suggests that there is a widespread interest in the fundamental questions of existence. Where are mankind from? Why is the universe the way it is?

This book set new standards for the presentation of complex physical relationships. In more recent editions, Steven Hawking has incorporated much of the knowledge and observational data that has come up since it was first published, on April first 1988: He wrote a new chapter on wormholes and time travel. Einstein's general theory of relativity seems to open up the possibility for him to create and use wormholes. They are small tubes that connect different regions of space/time.

And now Steven Hawking became a prophet: "If this were so, one day humans might be able to take lightning trips across the Milky Way!" Hawking was a smart fellow who knew the cosmic laws.

I landed on the Blue Planet through such a tube. It wasn't a lightning trip and it rocked quite a bit, as my crumpled suit showed only too clearly. For an 'earthling', this vision of a journey was a great dream of the future, albeit a little more complicated than he envisioned.

Professor Hawking also added to his debut work of popular science literature new reflections on the advances in the search for 'duality', or correspondences that have been achieved between seemingly disparate physical theories. These correspondences are strong evidence that there is a complete unified theory of physics.

However, these 'dualities' also suggest that it may not be possible to express this theory in a single fundamental formula. Instead, one may need to adhere to different aspects of the underlying theory in different situations. It's like not being able to map the surface of the planet Earth on a single map, but having to use different maps for different regions.

In this context, Steven Hawking comes to the conclusion that these considerations would be a revolution in the attitude towards the unification of scientific laws. Nevertheless, it would not change the most important point, that the universe is governed by a set of rational laws that can be discovered and understood.

The most important observational data for Hawking are the measurements of fluctuations in the cosmic microwave background by the Cosmic Background Explorer Satellite. These fluctuations are the fingerprint of creation, tiny irregularities in the otherwise regular and uniform universe. These irregularities later evolved into galaxies, stars, and all the other structures. This shape corresponds to the predictions of the hypothesis that the universe has no boundaries, or it has boundaries in the imaginary direction of time.

Professor Hawking wrote many other popular scientific works that were always successful. "I'm just a kid who never grew up. I keep brooding and still brooding over HOW- and WHY- questions. Sometimes I find an answer," he says, explaining his way of working.

Like Einstein, Hawking had an intelligence quotient of one hundred sixty. Although he snidely remarked that people who boast of a high IQ are losers. However, he was proud that he could think in eleven dimensions. Normal people are only limited to four dimensions, with the fourth dimension being time.

He also believed that extra-terrestrial life was quite common in the universe, but that intelligent life was much rarer. "Some say it has yet to appear on planet Earth," he added sarcastically.

In 2010, Hawking reflected on the possible risks that the search for extra-terrestrial life could pose to humanity. "If aliens ever visit us, I think like Christopher Columbus and his first arrival in America, it won't end well for native people." However, Steven Hawking saw the need for planet Earth to colonize space, but acknowledged that this would not be possible within a century.

In a series of lectures for the BBC in 2016, Hawking said that humanity was facing great dangers that threatened its very existence in the long term. So possible nuclear wars, genetically modified viruses, artificial intelligence (which evolves much faster than human abilities), and the climatic crises have the potential to wipe out humanity. The greatest danger to humanity is humanity itself. 'Homo hominis lupus est'.

"We run the risk of self-destructing out of greed and stupidity," was a grave warning. He also formulated positive thoughts: "Many people find the universe confusing – that's absolutely not true."

Hawking also had a sense of humor: "To ask what was before the universe began, is like asking what is north of the North Pole".

Or another quote with a laughing and a crying eye: "We are all just an evolved kind of apes, on an insignificant planet orbiting a very average star. But we can understand the universe. That makes us special."

Another quip that says a lot about Hawkins' understanding of the human soul: "Next time someone complains that you made a mistake, tell them that this could be a good thing. For without imperfection neither you nor I would exist."

Another quote from him: "I have noticed that people who believe in providence and that there is nothing we can do about it, still look left and right before they cross a road."

His mother once said in despair, "I wish Steven wasn't so wise and had a healthy body." That wish is only the right for a mother who believes she knows what is best for her child. Destiny has its own laws, and who can judge what makes another person happy, and what he is capable of, despite the greatest obstacles.

Hawking was a brilliant astrophysicist and his positive attitude despite a serious illness was admirable. He was optimistic, despite gloomy forecasts, he loved life. "Life would be tragic, if it wasn't funny."

"Remember to look up at the stars and down at your feet to make sense of what you see. And wonder what makes the universe exist. No matter how difficult life may seem, there is always something you can do and be successful at."

With his death, fifty-five years after his diagnosis, Hawking is considered the longest-surviving ALS patient to date. "I'm not afraid of death, but I'm in no hurry", was his attitude on the subject.

His ashes were buried in Westminster Abbey in London. His urn lies between the graves of Sir Isaac Newton and Charles Darwin. With his burial in Westminster Abbey, Hawking received the highest honor that can be bestowed on the Island of Britain for a famous scientist.

He popularized knowledge about the origin of the universe, black holes, the nature of time, intergalactic time travel and the search for the world formula in physics and cosmology, like no other scientist. He was a genius of the 21st century and truly a worthy exponent of the Cosmic Principle of Mentalism and Creation.

I wish I could have met Steven William Hawking on the Blue Planet!
   Lotus

Forth alpha-mail to Star Omicron 007
   Sent and received

The second Hermetic law – the Principle of Resonance – in the biography of Friedrich Schiller

"As above, so below, as below, so above. As within, so without, and as in great, so in small." Kybalion

The second Hermetic Principle states that everything a person experiences has a correspondence to him. All likes what he encounters shows what he is and what he thinks, what he feels, what he believes in. Every person you meet on an emotional level only expresses what is present within oneself.

According to these principles a poet can reach and touch the hearts of many humans when he formulates what his co-fellows only perceive vaguely as 'the beauty, the good and the truth'.

The literary work of Schiller represents resonance and correspondence. It is based on the idea that like attracts each other while unlike repels each other. Like-minded people find each other and attract people, things and thoughts that one desires in one's mind. It's important to monitor what you're thinking because the outside world will change accordingly.

Johann Christoph Friedrich Schiller, from 1802 'von' Schiller, (born 1759 in Marbach am Neckar, died 1805 in Weimar) was a medical doctor, poet, philosopher and historian. He is one of the most important German dramatists, poets and essayists.

With his theatrical debut, the play 'Die Räuber' (The Robbers), which premiered in 1782, Schiller made an important contribution to the 'Sturm und Drang' drama and world literature. This was understood as a fight for freedom against tyranny and also earned Schiller an honorary French citizenship. The reason for this honor was more Schiller's reputation as a rebel than his actual work – the resonance of his reputation preceded him.

Although Schiller was initially quite in favor of the French Revolution, he foresaw the turn from freedom resulting in the inhumane reign of terror of the Jacobins and detested the later mass executions in revolutionary France.

The drama 'Die Räuber' premiered at the national theater Mannheim. Public interest was great, since the printed edition that had appeared a year earlier had caused a stir because of its open criticism of the feudal system.

The performance caused a scandal. A contemporary witness reports: "The theater was like a madhouse, rolling eyes, clenched fists, hoarse screams in the auditorium. Strangers fell into each other's arms, sobbing, women staggered to the door on the verge of fainting. It was a general dissolution like chaos out of whose fog a new creation was emerging."

Schiller attended the premiere with a friend, although he was forbidden to do so. For this reason he had secretly left the 'Karlsschule' without asking for official permission. When, four months later, he traveled to Mannheim a second time without a holiday permit, Duke Carl Eugen put the insubordinate poet in arrest for fourteen days as punishment and prohibited him from any further contact with (kurpfälzisches Ausland) foreign countries.

The drama depicts the rivalry between two count brothers: on the one hand the intelligent, freedom-loving, later robber Karl Moor, loved by his father, and on the other hand, his coldly calculating brother Franz, suffering from lack of love, who is jealous of Karl and wants to usurp his father's inheritance. The central motif is the conflict between reason and feeling, the central theme is the relationship between law and freedom.

Schiller's dramas are visually powerful and eloquent, he does not shy away from crude expressions. "Franz is the name of the canaille!" But then also memorable sayings like: "Where there is a Brutus, there a Caesar must die."

Schiller's works were enthusiastically received not only in Germany but also in many other European countries. The response to the play 'The Robbers' reached as far as Japan and delighted audiences all over the world. The powerful and violent language and his feeling for the major current issues in society made Schiller particularly popular with younger and enthusiastic audiences.

With his dramas and literary-theoretical treatises, the poet intended to shape the aesthetic human being as a prerequisite for the non-violent transition to a rational state, and also as a counter-program to the French Revolution, as well as to contemporary politics, in which he saw only brute forces at work.

"The loveliest dreams of freedom are dreamed in prison." This is one of Schiller's many dictums, which like no other poet was able to trigger resonance in the hearts of his followers. It is said that many words must walk long before they become winged. Schiller began to write very early on. At the age of thirteen he wrote two plays, which unfortunately have not been preserved.

His first pamphlet on the philosophy of physiology (1779) was completely rejected by the experts – professors and personal physicians of Duke Carl Eugen, who was also present at the disputation. The reason given was that this work had too much 'fire'. This response was negative, but the response was there!

Schiller is a contemporary of the transition from the absolutist to the bourgeois era and the French Revolution. Since the bourgeoisie could not and was not allowed to express themselves politically under absolutism, which in Germany were often small states, literature became a central medium for increasing bourgeois self-confidence in the second half of the 18th century. Schiller's sensibility and his direct appeal to the most sacred feelings are an expression of the unfolding of the human, a principle opposed to the aristocratic lust for power.

"Oh, for free on all country maps
Are you looking for the blessed area,
Where freedom's evergreen garden,
There mankind blooms beautiful youth,"

(Ach umsonst auf allen Länderkarten
Spähst Du nach dem seligen Gebiet,
Wo der Freiheit ewig grüner Garten,
Wo der Menschheit schöne Jugend blüht.)

"Hallow is the ground beneath the tyrants, the days of their rule are numbered, and soon their trace will be no more to be found." (Hohl ist der Boden unter den Tyrannen, die Tage ihrer Herrschaft sind gezählt, und bald ist ihre Spur nicht mehr zu finden.)

"The old falls, time changes, and new life blooms from the ruins." (Das Alte stürzt, es ändert sich die Zeit, und neues Leben blüht aus den Ruinen.)

One of Friedrich Schiller's most famous works is the drama 'Don Carlos'. The poet wrote the work between 1783 and 1787 and published it under the full title 'Don Carlos, Infant von Spain', where it premiered in the same year. The play describes the events against the background of the eighty years war triggered by the Spanish occupation of the Netherlands.

The title character, Don Carlos, is the son of the Spanish King Philip II. whose reign lasted from 1556 to 1598. The prince, who was once very interested in politics, now devotes his entire attention to Elisabeth of Valois, with whom he is madly in love. However, his father, the king, married this woman in the meantime, which means that Elisabeth went from being his fiancée to Don Carlos' stepmother.

Against this background, Don Carlos and his childhood friend Marquis von Posa meet again. The confidante has returned from the Netherlands, where he was supposed to settle political conflicts. In order to prevent a threatening escalation there, the Marquis von Posa wants to persuade the prince to travel to the province of Flanders to mediate there. But Don Carlos has no interest in this and remains trapped in his unfortunate love madness, which also leads to his downfall.

The king realizes that resentment, intrigue and betrayal reign at court. In his search for trustworthy advisors, he comes across the Marquis von Posa. After initial hesitation, he agrees and becomes a minister and eventually a spy for the king. However, only on the surface, his heart only beats for his childhood friend Don Carlos.

When the situation becomes hopeless, the Marquis von Posa decides to sacrifice himself, which he eventually does. This shocks King Philip II. who regarded the Marquis as a confidante and held him in high esteem. In a conversation between the king and von Posa, the latter demands. "Give freedom of thoughts, Sire!" (Gebt' Gedankenfreiheit, Sire!)

This makes the Marquis von Posa the central character of the drama, because he fights for the rights of all human beings, not like Don Carlos only for his personal love. Schiller may have shifted the focus of resonance from the prince to the marquis while writing the drama, but retained the original title.

The core message of the drama is the constraints caused by social conventions. The possibilities of realizing oneself and one's personal goals are severely restricted by social guidelines and views. Freedom and tolerance are two essential demands of the Enlightenment era. Virtue and wisdom are found in this classic of German literature, embodied here by the Marquis von Posa.

When two geniuses live in the same era and in the same country, it is inevitable that they will resonate with each other. Before Schiller and Goethe became the legendary pair of friends of the Weimar classical period, who visited each other almost every day and exchanged not only literary, but also philosophical and scientific thoughts, they were competitors.

Goethe felt pressured by the younger man's growing fame. For him, Schiller was initially nothing more than an annoying reminder of his time in 'Werther' and his own 'Sturm und Drang' period, which he had since overcome.

And Schiller saw in the already well-established Goethe, who seemed unapproachable and arrogant when they first met, a 'proud prude who has to be made a child in order to humiliate her in front of the world'. What later connected the two previous rivals was their joint approach in their own work, in order to mutually support and improve one another. This was the declared purpose of their friendship.

This was a ten-year 'practical test of the educational idea in the classical period'. When Schiller died, an epoch came to an end for Goethe. The relationship had meanwhile become so intimate – despite fundamentally different values – that Goethe believed he would lose half his life, even himself, with Schiller's death.

Schiller was once invited to Weimar by Goethe in 1794 and spent two weeks in his house. He kept to his usual daily routine, that is, he slept until noon and worked at night. Knowing about Schiller's conservative morality, Goethe and his longtime partner Christiane Vulpius covered up their 'wild marriage'. Christiane and her five-year-old son remained invisible in their own home. Schiller described the relationship with Mademoiselle Vulpius as Goethe's 'only weakness'. He criticized him in a letter for his 'wrong notion about domestic bliss'. Goethe spoke of his 'marriage without ceremony'.

Schiller's passion for playing cards and tobacco bothered Goethe, who could sometimes be spiteful towards friends. The often-circulated anecdote that Schiller could only write poetry over the smell of rotten apples, also came from Goethe.

Friedrich Schiller died in Weimar in 1805 at the age of forty five from acute pneumonia. The mortal remains were finally transferred to the princely crypt in the new Weimar cemetery in 1827, where Goethe was later buried at his own request, 'at Schiller's side'.

Every classic period – albeit intense – ends up in a short time. It manifests, however, the peak of humanity.

In admiration of these two genius minds of the classical period.
Lotus

Fifth alpha-mail to Star Omicron 007
Sent and received

The third Hermetic law – the Principle of Vibration – in the biography of Laotse

"Nothing is still, everything moves, everything vibrates." Kybalion

The thoughts and ideas expressed by this philosopher can apply to all Hermetic Principles. Here, the Law of Vibration should be the focus of interest.

The whole universe is built like this, big and small. Spirit and matter face each other as polarities. The slow vibration of matter is easily perceptible, if a wheel rotates slowly, you can see the spikes. As speed increases, the spikes become invisible. Everything is permeated by vibrations, so everything is connected and can resonate.

The Tao Te King, attributed to Laotse, is a work in which the Tao – the Way – is described and followed by the appropriate course of action. Tao: means flow, principle and meaning; Te: refers to virtue, goodness, strength of character; King: is a guide, a canonical work. So the title is best left untranslated, an approximation would be: 'The Book of Tao and Its Power'.

A skeptical undertone prevails in this work. Laotse does not claim to have recognized and understood the way. In general, Laotse distrusts the human ability to perceive and to know. The sage does not proclaim his insights as incontrovertible truths. Thus, most chapters of the Tao Te King remain vague in their meaning and allow numerous interpretations. Parables follow ambiguous sayings.

That is why his teachings do not result in any strict rules, or even laws that prohibit certain actions. Laotse merely points out the consequences of certain actions, which may, or may not, be in harmony with the path. One example: "The violent do not die a natural death."

The ultimate goal is oneness with the Tao. The ideal image here is the 'unhewn block of wood', a metaphor that is often used. Tao is the path that leads to enlightenment, at the same time Tao is the origin of all beings and the unity of opposites. Quote: "The way is hidden, / but it is always present. / I don't know where he's from. / He is the original image of the origin of heaven."

Laotse is said to have lived at the time of the Spring and Autumn Annals in the 6th century B.C. in the southern State of Zhou. His family name is Li, which is more common in China than the German name Maier. His boyhood name was Erl (ear), his scholarly name was Be Yang (count, sun). After his death he was given the name Lao Dan (literally: old, long-eared; roughly translated: old teacher).

After spending a long time at the imperial court, which was then in Loyang (in today's Honan Province), as an archivist and practicing the Tao, Laotse sets off on a journey to the northwestern border of the Chinese Empire. When public conditions deteriorated to such an extent that order was no longer possible, Laotse wanted to withdraw from all offices.

The period was marked by wars and unrest, but also a heyday of Chinese philosophy. Many scholars wondered how peace and stability could be restored. It is said that Confucius visited Laotse to learn from him.

In order to escape the turmoil of time, Laotse is said to have retired to the solitude of the mountains. However, the border guard Yin Hi of the Han Gu mountain pass is said to have urged him not to withhold his wisdom from the world. Whereupon Laotse handed him the Tao Te King in eighty one verses, and five thousand ancient Chinese characters. Then Laotse went west, no one knows where. The legend that Laotse came into contact with Buddha in India is also linked to this story. The historical probability of this encounter is nearly zero.

Bertolt Brecht's thoughts are famous. In the 1920s and 1930s he studied the Tao Te King. He wrote his famous poem 'Legend of the origin of the book Tao Te King on the way of Laotse to the emigration', in the year 1938:

"When he was seventy and was frail
It urged the teacher to rest.
For the goodness in the country was once again weak
And the wickedness increased in strength once more
And he girded the shoes."

(Als er siebzig war und war gebrechlich
Drängte es dem Lehrer doch nach Ruh'
Denn die Güte war im Lande wieder einmal schwächlich
Und die Bosheit nahm an Kräften wieder einmal zu
Und er gürtete die Schuh.)

It then goes on to say that Laotse was stopped by a border guard who asked him to write down his teachings. After six days, the wise master finished it. Brecht's poem ends with the words:

"So thanks to the customs officer
He demanded it (the wisdom) from him."

(Darum sei der Zöllner auch bedankt
Er hat sie (die Weisheit) ihm abverlangt.)

In the Western world, Laotse is usually understood as a philosopher. The great attraction that Laotse exerts on Western people is also due to the fact that he gives the inexpressible, the elusive human mind, a placeholder, so to speak, a name – Tao.

There is no shortage of quotations attributed to Laotse. It often turns out, however, that there is nothing of the sort in the Tao Te King. This circumstance shows the probability that Laotse as individual, or as a group of old masters, knew and passed on shamanistic knowledge.

There are four forces in the universe: the people, the earth, the sky and the 'way'. One follows the other, only the path is a force in itself, following only its own nature. The way is a being that came before anything else, it is so big that it cannot be recognized. Although it created everything, it does not aspire to power and greatness.

51

Those who follow the Path do not need morals – they are inherently virtuous without having to make an effort. Morality results from the loss of the way, it is a stunted form of virtue that only leads to confusion. Their presence shows that trust and loyalty between people has been lost.

Everyone who follows the Path should guard three treasures: compassion, frugality and renunciation of fame. Only those who sympathize with others are courageous, only those who are frugal are generous, only those who do not seek fame and prestige can set an example and guide others.

The Way of Heaven is always a balancing act: Taking away from those who have too much, so that those who have too little may have enough. On the other hand, there is the way of the people: While some accumulate more and more possessions, others have less and less. Those who follow the Path of Heaven give away everything they don't need to survive.

The principle of vibration becomes particularly clear in the following thoughts: There is not much difference between two different points of view. Whether the answer is 'yes' or 'no' is mostly irrelevant. The truth often seems like a contradiction and usually doesn't sound nice. What sounds nice, on the other hand, is usually not true.

The sage never puts himself in the foreground, but takes himself back. Instead of harming others with words and deeds, he remains silent. By giving up himself, he is ahead of others; by forgetting himself he can find himself. The wise has little, empty himself and bows to others instead of excelling. Therefore he is recognized, honored and respected.

One doesn't have to travel far to learn about the world and understand the way. The further one goes out into the world, the less one sees. When the sage makes speeches, he points out mistakes without offending anyone.

Those who strive for inner emptiness and immerse themselves in silence return to their destiny and recognize the eternal. This enlightenment leads to righteousness and the Way of Heaven. True strength is shown by those who recognize themselves and overcome themselves. However, those who always desire more, conjure up their own judgement. Those who do violence to others stand against the Path.

The Tao Te King says about the unity of opposites: Only because we know the ugly can we appreciate the beautiful. The being emerges from the non-being, and all opposites are mutually interdependent. The Path unites all opposites. All things come down to it, and yet it needs neither possessions nor power, nor does it want to be thanked. Also people must unite opposites and seek unity. To do this, they must equally preserve male and female parameters, light and dark, honor and shame.

Only the interplay of opposites creates the things of this world. They all go back to the one way. That's why sometimes you win when you lose something; or you lose when you win something.

The nothing is just as important as the things that are there: A house only becomes habitable through the openings and thus through the emptiness. A vessel derives its usefulness from the hollow space inside. Therefore, what is not there is just as important as what is there.

Modesty is also advised in the Tao Te King, all excess inevitably leads to bad things: Those who have a lot are robbed, those who strive for high standing are disappointed. That's why it's better to only fill the glass half full, that means to remain humble. This corresponds to the Way of Heaven. Too much hectic and too many difficulties confuse the mind and the heart. You should be content with what you have.

He who prides himself, or boasts of his deeds will not gain fame or recognition from outside. Instead of putting on ornaments like fake kindness and fake resourcefulness, one should take an 'unhewn block of wood' as a model and live simply, plainly and frugally. Because the greatest crime is desire, the greatest evil is insufficiency, and the greatest misfortune is greed.

"Do you want to own the whole world? / Do you think you can make the world a better place? / I do not believe that is possible. / The universe is sacred just as it is. / You can't do better."

You can't improve the whole world because it's sacred just the way it is. Whoever tries to make the universe better will destroy it. In following the Path, one first realizes one's own virtue. Then the family, the village, the country and the whole world become virtuous.

The rulers should strive for simplicity and plainness and become like an 'unhewn wooden log'. If they do not interfere in the life of the people and do not give orders, they will be obeyed of their own accord. They too should not covet but seek stillness, so that peace and quiet can reign in the world.

A wise ruler is humble and puts himself aside instead of oppressing people. If he doesn't seek competition, he will have no competitors. Its inhabitants are content with what they have and do not aim far.

The rulers who do not follow the way accumulate treasures in their palaces while the people starve. They adorn themselves, squander and have more than they need. These rulers are no better than robbers. Instead of flattering the rulers with gifts, one should point them to the Path for their own sake and encourage them to be humble and frugal.

"The palace is full of treasures, / the fields are overgrown with weeds, / and the granaries are empty, / but the rulers wear splendid clothes (...) / this is certainly not the Way."

The Tao Te King also gives instructions for a planned life. Everything big has eventually emerged from something small, everything difficult was easy in the beginning. Therefore, one should tackle things while they are still small and simple. Planning ahead makes the work easier: A tree grows from a small seed, but eventually grows so big that no one can hold it. It's best to deal with things before they happen, and get things organized before they get mixed up. The wise recognizes difficulties before they arise and therefore does not face them in the first place.

Concerning the soft and the rigid, the Tao Te King emphasizes that human beings are soft when they are children, and plants are tender when they are young. But in old age and in death both become hard and rigid. So to be rigid is to be close to death, while the tender and yielding is closer to life. The soft gains victory. The best example is water: It is pliable and soft, yet it can gouge and move rocks. Although everyone knows that the soft is stronger than the hard in this sense, no one seems to conform to this idea.

The central theme of all political advice in the Tao Te-King is pacifism. According to Laotse, even if a country has an army, it would do well not to use it. Violence should only be used when you see no other option. The sections in which Laotse deals with armed violence and war are the only ones in which the philosopher, who otherwise strives so hard for balance and calm, shows excitement.

The renunciation of strife, violence and revenge is a virtue. Anyone who wants to lead others should have this virtue. If you are at war with another country, you should never launch an attack, but only defend yourself with a heavy heart. One can show strength even without weapons.

"Weapons are instruments of evil / and hated by all creatures. / Those who follow the Path / therefore do not insist on their use."

Despite this wise advice, the history of the Blue Planet is a history of wars, ever increasing in cruelty and irrationality.

Dearest Gowinda, more than ever the ideas of Laotse are disregarded on the planet Earth to detriment and impending annihilation.

I greet you with thoughtful thoughts,
    Your Lotus

Sixth alpha-mail to Star Omicron 007
    Sent and received!

Narcissism in the circle of family, partnership and children

Narcissism is an ubiquitous phenomenon: narcissistic parameters can be found everywhere, from fairy tales to serious crimes. The fairy tale of Snow White begins with the queen's wish: "If only I had a child as white as snow, as red as blood and as black as ebony." This shows the inner state of a woman with female-narcissistic personality traits.

The queen sits lonely at a window in the middle of winter and sews. The cold symbolizes a mental state of lethargy. The queen is alone and seems abandoned and lost. The work she does – sewing – is not worthy of her.

The time of the big celebration on the occasion of her wedding is over. The queen has grown humble, accompanied by a sense of inferiority and depression. The window's ebony frame symbolizes a somber part of her life. However, in this point in time, the middle of winter already indicates a turning point. It cannot go on like this.

The event of the needle prick brings movement into the lethargy, which is enlivened by the desire for a child. Even now, the mother-to-be has a clear idea of how the girl should be: her skin as white as snow, her lips red as blood, and her hair black as ebony. The girl should correspond to the ideal that the mother designs. In addition, the child should free the mother from her emotional distress and give her existence a meaning.

The mother does not love the child as it is, but the image of it. It serves as a narcissistic extension of the mother. The situation of the child is characterized by narcissistic exploitations. Because for the mother the girl has to sacrifice its own liveliness and autonomy.

Blood, snow and the ebony frame take on a new meaning: the blood as a symbol of sacrifice, the snow as a the lethargy from which the child is supposed to free the mother, and the frame as a symbol for the image of the child who is loved more than even the child.

This initial situation is characteristic of the childhood and youth of later narcissistic people. Two parameters play an important role in this: Narcissistic exploitation and narcissistic extension. Exploitation includes gaining individual benefits from another person.

The child increases the self-esteem of the parents. In principle, this is not negative as long as the appreciation of the parents does not come at the expense of the child and its individuality. But it's certainly not right when a child needs to nurture and stabilize its parents emotionally, rather than the other way around.

A child is then exploited when it is supposed to have certain qualities and abilities for the parents, even if they are against its nature. A girl cannot become a boy, because the parents wanted a heir to preserve the name of the family. This is probably one of the most glaring examples, which is not that rare, even though there is no kingdom to be inherited.

These desires and demands on the child often exist before it is born. They shape the parent's attitude towards their child, depending on how well it meets their expectations. If the deviations are very large, the child will be confronted with their disappointments. The parents then try to change the child through control and punishment. But such a child can almost never meet the expectations of the parents. The wound of not being loved, the way it is, remains.

Narcissistic adults will later exploit other people just as they were exploited as children. They choose friends and partners based on the extent to which they serve their own narcissistic needs. These people are usually not loved for their own sake, but because of their position, their achievements, or their material wealth.

Narcissistic extension means that the parents extend themselves through the child, and the adult woman through the partner, by adopting their abilities. If the child is bright, happy and successful in school, the parents can identify themselves with these qualities. Praise and admiration received by the child are valued by the parents. They love it all the more, the more recognition they gain from the child. But this love is more a form of admiration, because it relates less to the child as it is, and more to its positive qualities and its achievements.

The fairy tale of Snow White also tells of other narcissistic disorders: The stepmother's competition for beauty and youth, although the king and father plays no role in this story. At seven years old, Snow White is a thousand times more beautiful than the royal stepmother, according to her magic mirror. With that, her death is a done deal. The queen takes her competition to the point of cannibalism. She eats the heart and liver of the animal, which the hunter cheatingly brings to the queen as proof of Snow White's killing.

This fairy tale is about the motive that the mother does not want the daughter to develop and grow up. The girl suffocates in her mother's obsession with beauty. On the way to independence, Snow White returns to the world of childhood.

In expressions like little table, little cup, little bed, the language indicates the regression. Since the girl refuses to take steps towards maturity, she doesn't recognize her stepmother's malice and ends up in a glass coffin: A symbol for being buried alive. Those affected are alive, they are not clinically dead, they feel an inner emptiness and only take part in life at a great distance. They no longer feel themselves and have lost contact with themselves and other people.

The glass coffin can also have another meaning: It symbolizes passivity, expecting change from the outside. The others, parents, siblings and friends suffer with her, just like the dwarfs weep for Snow White.

The tripping of the pallbearers and the fall that causes Snow White to vomit up the poisoned apple and comes back to life, represents the fact that the environment is ceasing to relieve Snow White of the responsibility for solving her own problems.

Then she has to start growing up and becoming responsible for herself. Only when she no longer expects her partner to satisfy her desires can she enter into a healthy relationships, not to be a doll, but a loving woman.

Such complex and diverse disorders as narcissism cannot be traced back to individual causes. Narcissism is not hereditary, but there are many factors that increase susceptibility within the family. This is about dispositions or vulnerabilities that relate to physical, psychological and/or social factors.

However, the rapid increase in narcissistic behaviors in Western society in recent decades also proves that these personality disorders cannot be hereditary, because genes do not change that quickly. Basically, there are two models for the development of narcissism within a family: An improper level of emotional support in childhood, too much, or too little.

The myth of Narcissus already tells of the admiring mother, who spoiled the boy, coddled him, cleared all difficulties out of the way and thus gave no structure and sense of responsibility, and did not develop these qualities in the child either.

The child can never learn to endure stress, manage frustration, or deal with hurt properly. Confronted with problems later, strategies for solving them are lacking. Everything is interpreted as a personal attack and felt as an insult. The child thus becomes overly sensitive and develops a skin that is too thin for the often rough storms of life. This explains the excessive sensitivity of the narcissist.

At the same time, a child brought up in this way likes to play the star role, which he gets through false encouragement, false praise and the fulfillment of every wish. Even later, as an adult, it will always strive to be the center of attention and live it out in an uncompromising way. This attitude of entitlement, encouraged by the parents, is later extended to the entire environment. This person demands without ever thinking of anything in return. The wrong programming for uniqueness carried out in childhood leads to the lifelong error, the claim to one's own and special privileges.

This unreal lifestyle – often with the best of intentions – has serious side effects. The spoiled child does not see its parents as independent personalities with needs of their own. The opposite, the 'you' disappears behind the pampering attitude. The parents don't give any structure, no buffer and no security. They show too few of their own feelings for which the child can build up emotional resonance. This explains why narcissists have so little empathy and can hardly show appreciation and affection for their partners, families and friends.

A coddling upbringing robs the child of a lot of independence and initiative. Since the parents act out their needs in the child, it does not get to know its own desires and talents. It feels vulnerable and dependent. In this way, the child is pushed into a development in which one only relies on oneself and does not need other people at all.

The second hypothesis sees the main cause of narcissistic disorders not in too much, but in too little emotional attention. It is not the spoiling, but the undersupply of love and feelings that leads to narcissism. Every child has a basic need for positive emotions. In addition to physical care, it needs the closeness and security of its parents. It wants to be noticed and loved by everyone it relates to, mother, father, siblings, relatives.

The child panics when these core needs are not met. It will try by any means necessary to get what is being denied. If a narcissist expresses intense desires for approval and admiration – even without any reason – this can be interpreted as a cry for the love denied in childhood. This narcissistic force to compel approval is immense and difficult to understand.

So the drama of the narcissist begins with the drama of the parents. These promote their own needs onto the children through projections. Due to their own emotional deficits and wrong upbringing, narcissistic disorders develop in the children. Behind a gorgeous exterior hides an emotionally bedraggled, desperate child who hungers for recognition and reflection of his true identity.

The human need for reflection is currently shown in the heavy use of social media. This mirror function (selfies, likes or dislikes) serves the same human need to build one's identity as interpersonal mirroring does. It is the shine in the mother's eye that makes the child happy.

Relationships with mother and father are different. On the one hand, the daughter is closely related to the mother because of the same sex, on the other hand, she rejects her because she is so powerful. Often the daughter also has to take on the role to 'mother' the mother, satisfying her needs and filling inner emptiness. But the daughter also does not release her mother from her supportive function either. So both are chained together, believing that neither can live and exist without the other. Then dependency, addiction, fears and depressions arise.

Another fictional scenario shows a woman who desperately wants to live within the framework of a family, be it because of her own conviction, or because of her parent's wishes. The whole family, the 'sacred cow', was the ideal of the 19th century and the desired way of life until the middle of the 20th century. The fact that at least one parent suffers mentally and physically to the point of collapse, while maintaining a toxic family structure, the children osmotically – even without words – grasp that a lot is wrong, is accepted as collateral damage. There is a high probability that the same game will be repeated in the next generation, with the children playing the role of perpetrators or victims.

The relationship with the father is also characterized by contradictions and opposites. He is the other, different from the mother, embodying activity and exploration. It becomes particularly important when the child is to evolve away from the family and integrate into a peer group. This is much more difficult for young people who have grown up without a father, where the threesome relationship does not exist.

The daughter perceives the physical, but also the emotional absence of the father as a rejection. If she senses her father's withdrawal during puberty, she tries all the more to win his favor. This relationship pattern to the father may be the basis for a narcissistic woman's lifelong search for approval from a man. This results in a lack of self-confidence, a feeling of inadequacy. In her partner she is looking for her lost father and his unconditional love.

The seductive behavior of narcissistic people implies that they were treated the same way as children. So they will continue the seductive behavior when dealing with men. These women tend to sexualize their relationships or allow a man to exploit them sexually.

The narcissistic father's attitude, physical and/or emotional absence, unconcerned about his children's education, and failure to even consider professional jump-start, are burdens that weigh heavily on any relationship with children and their ability for bonding. If this trend continues, the term 'father' could become a 'dirty word'.

Often a father has no interest in the development of his children, whose cry for attention and affection disturbs his hobbies, mostly computer games (or other addictions). He indulges in his digital dementia: It has been scientifically proven that staring at the screen for hours every day, which includes hearing and seeing, causes permanent changes in the brain and a loss of reality.

If a narcissistic mother has had little education, and also has no insight that one could catch up later, the situation for the children is particularly precarious. There is probably not much positive to report about her family of origin. It probably belongs to a lower social drawer in which education, culture and art have little value. If she doesn't even master her own mother tongue and only speaks in a broad dialect, decorated with case errors, their children will have a hard time, especially when learning any foreign language.

This mother would not have to catch up on high school, let alone aiming for a university degree. However, she should recognize her deficits, if only for the benefit of her children. She should at least read books, learn a foreign language and be interested in something that goes beyond her own nose.

As a narcissist, she behaves like a peacock, but since she is not male, she cannot make a cartwheel with one hundred fifty colorful feathers, but only spread her gray feathers, and make a fool of herself. She wants to play the grandiose narcissist and even has the audacity to accuse her son's partner of not raising children in a right way. It is obvious that such a mother cannot properly prepare her children for life.

The current digital development offers even more possibilities to be narcissistic. Showing up virtually might be easier for people with low self-esteem than showing up in face-to-face relationships. In extreme cases, virtual communication can even replace face-to-face encounters. Showing yourself, as you are, means taking the risk of not pleasing. But to please is the narcissistic primary goal.

Such an attitude opens the floodgates to self-optimization. Those who always want to get better find it difficult to find satisfaction in the present reality. But that strengthens the feeling of inferiority, especially in women, who compensate for this with narcissistic exaggerations. Then inner emptiness and mental hunger arise, which are filled with material goods. This leads to an alienation from one's own being in favor of an illusory world that neither makes one sated nor happy.

The globalization of the digital system has also developed new forms of crime, which are only possible to this extent through narcissistic disorders, both in criminal perpetrators and in love-hungry victims. The many dating platforms are the prerequisite for 'Love killing'. People looking for love and attention are mercilessly ripped off.

'Love killers' are good psychologists and strategists, they choose their victims carefully. The majority of those active in Germany come from West Africa, especially Ghana. After carefully analyzing the profiles of possible candidates, they send fake photos of Caucasian people and eloquently chat about love clichés.

They can estimate exactly how long it takes for each individual case until the victim is hooked and emotionally bound. Sometimes it even comes to a long-distance marriage. The current digital technology makes the impossible possible. On average, it takes a month of daily chatting. Then something dramatic happens unexpectedly. These 'gentlemen' know exactly which scam works with which victims:

- a family member, often a mother or brother, urgently needs an operation;
- a bomb-deal has almost burst and requires another large investment to save it;
- a lawyer must be paid urgently, otherwise the process is lost;
- an one-time good investment in promising securities or stocks would be possible (for those victims who are particularly greedy);
- there are certainly other credible variants, if one wants to believe it.

The justification of such a narcissistic 'robber baron' is interesting: "Sometimes I feel sorry for them – the victims – especially when they have lost everything, including the house they lived in. But not very. After all, the Europeans enslaved us and stole our country's natural treasures. Now we're taking it back from the women."

The psychological skill of these adventurers, who feel justified in making criminal capital out of feelings, expectations and hopes, is remarkable. They operate from a distance, mostly by telephone, with Skype calls there are always technical problems with image and sound. They communicate with a culture that is foreign to them, in a foreign language, mostly English with a few scraps of German. Despite all these obstacles, they create an accurate psychogram of their victims. But this also shows that basic human needs are the same all over the world. Narcissism is a colorful phenomenon and includes criminal greed and hunger for love.

Men are ripped off by the same system. Here the number of unreported cases is much higher than for women, shame prefers silence.

During the pandemic, this type of crime increased by 35% in Germany. In this country, the official annual damage sum has risen to over two million Euro. The average was twenty thousand Euro, but often significantly more. Narcissistic tendencies can get expensive when you mistake dreams for reality.

As with many mental disorders, biological explanations are now being sought for narcissism. There is one scientific study that is worth mentioning: In narcissists, the brain regions responsible for family and social thinking, as well as for empathy, show less volume and substance. However, it is unclear whether this disorder is congenital, or whether the social areas atrophy through self-centered and selfish behavior.

Although narcissistic disorders appear to have a certain recurrence in family histories, no genetic marker for these disorders has been identified. In contrast to narcissism, malfunctions in the brains metabolism could be observed in anxiety disorders and depression. The neurotransmitters are not imbalanced in narcissists. Therefore, one cannot expect any success from psychotropic drugs. In short, there is no pill against narcissism!

To be continued,
Marta

Seventh alpha-mail to Star Omicron 007
Sent and received

The fourth Hermetic law – The Principle of Rhythm – in the biography of Martha Graham

"Everything flows in and out, everything has its tides, all things rise and fall, the swing of the pendulum is evident in everything, the measure of the swing to the right is the measure of the swing to the left. Rhythm compensated." Kybalion

Martha Austin Graham was an American dancer, choreographer and dance teacher (1894 – 1991). She is recognized by professionals as an innovator of modern American dance in which the rhythm of breath and movement plays a central role. Everything flows in and out, everything has its tides, all things rise and fall and can thus express emotions through dance.

Martha Graham has been called the 'Picasso of dance' in that her impact on modern dance is synonymous with Picasso's on modern visual art. Her influence has also been compared to that of Stravinsky on music and Frank Lloyd Wright on architecture.

She was the person who brought dance into the 20th century. She revolutionized classical ballet by no longer subordinating the forms of dance to a standardized movement sequence, but giving unconditional priority to feeling, emotion and rhythm over movement. In ever new attempts at self-exploration, she built her range of dance techniques on the elementary components of tension and relaxation, as well as breathing.

"People asked me why I became a dancer. I didn't choose, I was chosen to be a dancer. That's how I've lived my whole life." This is her commitment to dance. The Martha Graham technique is characterized by powerful, dynamic, rugged and tense movements. Graham's ballet art was also inspired by a variety of cultural influences such as modern painting, the American pioneer era, aborigines religious ceremones and Greek mythology.

She worked with artists of other origins, composers, sculptors and fashion designers who participated in her projects. Classical ballet stars such as Margot Fonteyn and Rudolf Nureyev danced in her pieces. In her more than 60 years of stage work, Graham created over 180 works. At the age of 76 she gave her last dance performance with great regret. She was still choreographing her dance pieces at the age of 96 years.

For Martha Graham, dance is "the hidden language of the soul and body. Great dancers are not great because of their technique. They are great because of their passion." According to her own interpretation, her method of movement was based on breathing and impulse control, which she called 'contraction and relaxation'. For her, movement originated in the tension of a contracted muscle and follows the flow of energy coming out of the body. Tension and relaxation is the basis of Graham's dance style. This is in contrast to the technique of classical ballet, which aims to create an illusion of weightlessness. "For me, the body can express what words cannot." For Martha Graham dancers are messengers of the gods.

Graham turned away from classical ballet because she wanted dance to be an art form that resided in the vulnerability of human experience rather than as a form of entertainment. This motivated her to omit the more decorative movements of ballet and emphasize the fundamental aspects of movement.

Her style of choreography was dramatic. Often the vibrancy and intensity of her intent was so strong that the curtain rose like a thunderclap. At that moment you had to decide whether you were 'for' or 'against' her. She radicalized her movements to such an extent that they were devoid of any external substance and focused on the highest concentration.

She also stated: "Dance seems glamorous, relaxed and delightful. But the road to the paradise of achievement is no easier than any other."

For Martha Graham "dance is poetry. It's like poetic lyricism, sometimes it's like the harshness of dramatic poetry, it's like terror – or it can be like a terrifying realization of a truth. Because when you illuminate a single word, it goes straight to your heart."

"The only thing that matters is that one moment in the movement. Make this moment important, alive and worth living. Don't let it slip away unnoticed and not needed." For Graham, dance is an expression of 'inner music, the hidden language of the soul'.

She took a psychoanalytic view of dance. She thought that the purpose of dance was to illuminate life, the struggles of human existence with a special emphasis on the inner nature of man.

"We look at dance as a means of expressing the feeling of living in the affirmative; to give the viewer a heighten awareness of the power, mystery, humor, greater diversity and wonder of life. That is the function of American dance."

The Principle of Rhythm also includes the fact that there is no standstill, that everything changes. Everything has a beginning, a climax and an end. This is often difficult for people to accept. Martha Graham fell into severe depression when she was no longer able to perform on stage.

This was in 1970 when she was 76 years old. "When I stopped dancing, I lost my will to live. I locked myself at home, ate little, drank too much and brooded. My face was ruined and people said I looked weird, which I can only agree with. Finally I broke down. I was in the hospital for a long time, mostly in a coma."

She adds later: "It was only many years after I left ballet that I could bear to see someone else dance. I believe in the principle of never looking backwards, not burying yourself in nostalgic thoughts and memories. However, how can you avoid it when you look onto the stage and see a dancer performing what you yourself accomplished 30 years ago: Creating a ballet with someone you loved deeply, your husband? I think this is what Dante left out in the circles of hell."

With this statement, Martha Graham refers to her brief marriage with a dancer who was the first male member to appear briefly in her dance company, the Martha Graham Center of Contemporary Dance. Here, the Principle of Rhythm ended her hope for a long, happy community. Sometimes fate has to break a person before healing can happen.

Martha Graham not only recovered from her breakdown, she surpassed herself. Having sunk into the deepest abyss, she began a new cycle of life. In 1972 she quit drinking, returned to her studio, reorganized her dance company and choreographed ten new ballets and many revivals. She completed her last ballet in 1990, 'Maple Leaf Rag'.

During her lifetime, Graham received many national and international awards. She was the first dancer to perform in the White House, traveled the world as a cultural ambassador, and received America's highest civilian honor, the Presidential Medal of Freedom with Distinction. Other honors include 'the Key to the City of Paris', the Danish Medal of Merit, 'Japan's Imperial Order of the Precious Crown', et cetera.

In 1998, Martha Graham was posthumously named 'Time Magazine's Dancer of the Century' and 'People's Female Icon of the Century'. In 2015 she was posthumously inducted into the 'National Women's Hall of Fame'.

A student of Martha Graham, a dancer, and a physiotherapist developed a new movement method based on Graham's findings: 'Antara'; this is a Sanskrit word meaning 'from the inside out'. And that's exactly what it's all about, 'Antara' acts on the deep muscles.

A few years ago scientists discovered that the human skeleton is essentially supported by an inner corset of muscles, the core muscles. These include the diaphragm, the transversus, i.e. the transverse abdominal muscles and the pelvic floor. This corset becomes slack as a result of everyday incorrect posture, such as sitting down for a long time, but also standing up for a long period. In conventional gymnastics, however, only the outer muscles are trained. 'Antara' tries to bring the corset back to its original pattern.

About 200 years ago, the armchair was introduced for the general public and with it began a sitting culture from school to all white-collar professions. When yoga was developed thousands of years ago, people were still moving a lot because they lived from agriculture and animal husbandry. Nothing has changed in the movement sequences in traditional yoga and therefore it no longer corresponds entirely to the physiological needs of modern people.

The same is true, to a lesser degree, with Pilates, which was originally developed by Joseph Pilates some 70 years ago, for war invalids, but then popularized by dancers in America who valued the rhythmic character and use of breathing to enhance the possibility of expression.

In this way, 'Antara' combines the latest scientific findings with proven elements of movement, breathing, rhythm of tension and relaxation as well as the morphological needs of modern people in their sitting culture.

I love and admire the personality and life of Marta Graham. In the future I will increase my dancing sessions.

Marta

Eighth alpha-mail to Star Omicron 007
    Sent and received

Narcissism in the mirror of gender

Narcissism is predominantly male, narcissistic personality disorder affects – within the total population – more than half of the sad male patients. Oh, those affected do not feel themselves sad, mostly grandiose. But that doesn't last forever.

According to scientific findings, men are less empathetic, more aggressive, have more assertiveness and have lower social sensitivity. In addition, the heroes of mankind are more active, competitive, confident and commit far more crimes than women. These and other traits are a strong breeding ground for narcissism and explain the asymmetry in the distribution of this disorder.

Male and female narcissism differs not only quantitatively, but also qualitatively. A Cristiano Ronaldo is typically male, it's hard to imagine a woman appearing like that. At the age of twenty two he published the book 'Moments' about the highlights of his career so far. At the age of twenty eight he opened his own museum in his hometown of Funchal. Significantly, Ronaldo called the film about himself, financed by millions from him: 'The world at his feet'. Even the somewhat more modest statement of a former Austrian finance minister, '... he is too beautiful, too intelligent and too rich ...' will hardly ever come from the lips of a woman.

The term narcissist is first associated with a certain type of man: machos who establish relationships through seduction, who have to retain power over their partner and, if things could get serious, end the relationship.

On the outside, they are often arrogant and aggressive people. They always want to be the center of attention and also see their partners as an audience that should make their lives more beautiful and comfortable. They're oozing with self-esteem that needs no justification. Additionally, they exaggerate the value of their accomplishments, talents and expect to be recognized as superior.

Narcissists indulge in fantasies of their success and power, believing in all seriousness that they are special and unique. A male narcissist needs excessive admiration like air to breathe. He has an amazing sense of entitlement and expects special benefits.

He tries to exploit everyone who comes into contact with him to achieve his own goals. He is calculating and exploiting every human relationship. This shows his attitude towards everyone. The narcissist is often jealous because he believes that the success of others is unjustified. Conversely, he easily interprets that others are jealous of him.

In personal relationships, he shows himself to be dismissive, unreachable for the wishes of his partner, little empathetic and emotional. These are typical characteristics of the grandiose male narcissist.

Female narcissists resemble the description above. They appear confident, cool and superior. They often operate with seduction, both with men and women, because they have learned to quickly adjust to the expectations and desires of other people.

This is where the difference between male and female narcissists becomes apparent. While men fight for their autonomy, women adapt in hopes of gaining their partner's approval and affection. Adaptation can go as far as self abandonment.

The male type emphasizes the distance, which he experiences as autonomy. He can be trapped in computer games for hours, simply ignoring or even forgetting his wife and children. Essentially a 'relationship avoidant', he resists a real relationship and seems content with himself.

The female type, on the other hand, reacts by over-adapting and giving up her own identity. They are clingy in relationships, but are just as incapable of real adjustment as the male type. They belong to the group of 'relationship seekers'.

But there are also numerous men who have a female-narcissistic personality structure, i.e. they correspond more to the clinging type. The childhood experience of these men is often shaped by a mother who exploits the son as a piece of jewellery. The son should make the mother happy and/or save her from her mental distress.

In this way, the child learns, early on, to focus its attention on other persons. He lacks the father as support and structure, because he is either absent or unavailable for the son, even when he is physically present. This lays the seeds for a basic sense of inferiority.

Conversely, there are also women who live more the male-grandiose version of narcissism. Both forms, male and female, have the same basic narcissistic disorder of hurt self-esteem. In their interactions, they each show a different side: the female type 'clinging' and the male type 'avoiding'. But under the grandiose facade of the vain rooster lies a depression, and behind the depressive mood of the narcissist female lies the grandiosity.

The different manifestations of female and male narcissism are related to the socialization of gender and the role models of women and men have in society. For thousands of years, boys and men have been overestimated and girls and women have been degraded to second-class status. This manifests itself in the collective unconsciousness and influences people's behavior.

Girls are seldom encouraged to assert themselves aggressively, while boys are expected to behave this way. Boys should defend themselves when attacked, be strong and manly. Red Indians don't cry. And that's how a narcissistic man behaves.

The narcissistic conflict consists in the incompatibility of two extreme poles of experience: grandiosity and inferiority. In Western culture, women seem to be more at the pole of inferiority and men more at the pole of grandiosity. There are many mixed types, but under stress everyone resorts to their preferred defense mechanisms: Men make themselves even more grandiose, women feel even more worthless.

In order to maintain the outward image of a competent woman, they take on masculine traits. This is reflected in a more rational than emotional attitude. Everything becomes feasible and controllable. This masculine attitude becomes the ideal to which women conform. But appearances are often deceptive. Behind this self-confident behavior there is often an emotionally clingy woman who fears criticism and rejection from her partner.

In the pioneering work 'Female Narcissism', by Bärbel Wardetzki (2021), a comparison of the two basic patterns of narcissistic disorders is developed. The most important parameters are described below.

While the male narcissist emphasizes his grandiosity, a sense of inferiority and depression appears in the female narcissist. He upgrades and makes himself unassailable, while she makes herself small and a victim.

He fights for admiration and autonomy. She wants recognition through adaptation to the point of self-abandonment. He compensates for his weaknesses with grandiosity, she with performance and attractiveness. He is distant and derogatory, she is empathetic and compassionate to the point of taking on someone else's feelings. He's a narcissist, she's a co-narcissist.

He never gives himself up in a relationship, while she submits. He stabilizes his self-esteem through his partner and her admiration. She borrows an idealized self from the partner and his professional success. He seeks a mother figure, she seeks a father figure and mothers him. While he behaves aggressively and dismissively, she chooses the passive form of aggressiveness: denial and defiance. He assumes a persecuting position, withdrawing to the point of breaking up, while she wards off offense through harmonization and adjustment.

In the already classic work 'Men are different, Women too' (1992), the author John Gray describes the difference between the sexes very aptly: Men are like rubber bands, women are like waves.

Men oscillate between closeness and autonomy. When they move away, they only go a certain distance and then come back with momentum. The rubber band is a perfect image to describe the male way of dealing with intimacy. A man needs his cave to satisfy his need for independence. If he seems very far away, he will feel the need for closeness again. You should understand this game and not follow the man into his cave.

For women who feel loved, their confidence rises and falls like waves. When a woman's wave rises, she feels filled with love. When it falls she feels an emptiness inside, she finds herself in a deep hole. During this time it is important for her to talk to her partner or friend about her problems, to be heard and understood. She doesn't want to hear solutions or minimization of her problems. With the knowledge of the different strategies of men and women, many tears and insults could be avoided.

The role of women is subjected to cultural and social changes. Developments in the 1960s and 1970s opened up new areas for women to be independent in their jobs, and to organize their lives individually. However, these new possibilities were now added to their previous tasks.

The conventional image of women has expanded. The traditional housewife role is no longer in demand, but the attractive working woman who takes care of the household, husband and children, the charming hostess and supporter of the partners career.

This can easily lead to being overwhelmed, which is why women must be careful not to neglect their needs in addition to their role as partner and not to define themselves solely through being a mother. It is almost impossible to cover this large area of responsibility evenly if the partner does not contribute significantly. But how often and how long does this take place?

What did the suffragettes bring to women? The right to vote, which they can exercise every four, five or six years. And in the meantime, they're struggling to the point of self-abandonment.

In ancient times, women were sex objects that were bought, cherished, and cared for at great expense. Later, the majority of the female population lived in an employment relationship, but had to be at the will of their masters. But at least, they got paid.

The modern woman has to finance herself in marriage, give birth to and raise children, contribute financially to the household and usually organize it on her own. She has often also to bring in the constant financial support of her parents. Although she contributes financially to the rent, she is only listed as a sub-tenant on the registration form. And when the children have moved out, the woman is left with the role of an unpaid house-keeper. The sexual component has long since ceased to exist. Progress has strange facets!

Let's turn to more kind topics: The fairy tale of Cinderella is also about narcissism and its overcoming. There is a struggle between inferiority – Cinderella – and grandiosity – the stepsis-ters and their mother. In the sisterly rivalry conflict, Cinderella is exposed to the arbitrariness and ridicule of her stepsisters.

But Cinderella is supported by the tree she planted on her mother's grave, the little bird and the doves. Even if her own mother is dead, she experiences salvation through her. This in-dicates a good bond between mother and child that survives even death. This can mean the realistic death of the mother, or her inability to assert herself against the father, who does not take Cinderella's side.

Cinderella is the one who is not like the others. The expe-rience of being left out, of not being loved, is the result. She does not live as she should, but instead in forced humiliation. She puts herself in the position of the wallflower that nobody loves. It doesn't matter who the devaluation comes from. What matters is the pain.

The poor girl does not rebel but endures her situation, until the day of the celebration of the bride's choice feast, the symbol of her becoming a wife. She really wants to be there, but is re-jected because she is supposed to sort out lentils from the ashes.

Lentils are a female symbol of fertility, and tossing them in the ashes means destroying Cinderella's femininity. By collect-ing the good lentils in the pot, she regains herself. But again and again, she is prevented from developing.

The turning point comes with the help of the deceased moth-er, who sends her a wedding dress so that she can attend the king's feast. But everything has to be done in secret: The stepsisters are not allowed to see her, she has to be back before midnight, otherwise her chance is wasted.

Many women with narcissistic personality disorder live in secrecy, because they don't trust themselves to face the daylight. They are afraid that their masquerade will be recognized and exposed. They believe that others are better, more lovable, more valuable. They then take refuge in the role of inferiority.

The stepmother's refusal to introduce Cinderella to the prince is symbolic of the woman's fear of showing her inferior parts. This is often overcompensated by grandiosity. This does not happen with Cinderella. However, this modesty can become a problem when women don't take hold of the gift which is offered. But when women trust their feelings – when doves are involved – symbols of wisdom and love – they allow themselves to be chosen.

In the end, neither grandiosity nor inferiority wins. No mutilations, no manipulation of the body (cutting off the heel and toe to fit the shoe), no outward alteration can redeem her from inferiority. This can only happen when she is authentic and experiences her true worth in a healthy relationship where she is allowed to be as her nature is.

Narcissism is not found in ancient psychology. Galen of Pergamon developed the four temperaments: sanguine, choleric, melancholic and phlegmatic. All four temperaments may, or may not have, narcissistic traits. Sigmund Freud was the first to place the topic of narcissism at the center of psychology, psychiatry and psychotherapy.

However, only the systematics of the geneticist and psychotherapist, Robert Gloninger, allowed an assignment of the personality disorder and thus of narcissism. These thoughts are clearly presented in the work by R. Bonelli, 'Male Narcissism' (2018).

Gloninger calculated the four dimensions of temperaments from his immense pool of data. The progress of this work consisted in the genetic and neurobiological validation of the typologies. As part of his assignment of temperaments to neuroanatomical structures, the scientist discovered that the four dimensions of temperament represent the phylogenetically oldest areas of the brain. Therefore, he also worked out properties of the phylogenetically younger brain areas, namely the frontal and temporal neocortex.

Only the difference of these brain areas differentiates 'homo sapiens' from apes. Gloninger called the characteristics located there, in contrast to innate temperament, the 'three dimensions of character'. These are self-control, cooperation, and self-transcendence. The parameter 'self-control' distinguishes 'reliable and objective' from 'blaming and haphazard'. Ability to cooperate refers to characteristics such as 'helpful, tolerant, team player' in contrast to 'vindictive, criticism-resistant and prejudiced'. Self-transcendence emphasizes 'spiritual values' over 'I, more I, most I', and materialistic values.

Self-control corresponds to the inner order of a human being, the ability to cooperate is the order in relationships, and self-transcendence corresponds to the integration of the human being into a cosmic whole.

If you analyze a 'self-loving rooster' in the mirror of the 'three dimensions of character', the narcissist tends to tip over into accusing others instead of being factual and reliable. In relationships, he tends to be vengeful, less team-oriented and less helpful. Finally, a 'vain peacock' is certainly more self-centered than self-less. Gloninger's concept also shows that narcissistic behavior is less related to innate temperament than to acquired character. So you are not born as a narcissist.

But every human being has narcissistic parts in it, certainly in gradations. The same symptoms are present in 'Herr Jedermann's microscopically – often also macroscopically. In Hugo von Hofmannsthal's play, everyday ruthlessness, which 'Herr Jedermann' considers to be insignificant collateral damage to a comfortable life, is presented almost unnoticed at first. The 'good deeds' are chronically neglected and are 'frail' in need of support. With Hofmannsthal, the story has just a happy ending. But only after a life-threatening crisis and shocking self-awareness.

The narcissistic man doesn't believe that he has to be special for everyone to be loved, admired and appreciated. He is totally convinced that he is special and that it's his legitimate right that he is always the center of attention and affection. Oscar Wilde once pointed out in relation to his own life: "Love of yourself is the beginning of a lifelong romance". But that can lead to an uncomfortable and painful crash landing.

In the cultural history of mankind, narcissism does not get good marks. Religion and philosophy have been critical of arrogance and pride for thousands of years. As early as the 6th century B.C., Laotse states, "He who boasts is not trusted. He who is proud of himself is not a lord." He goes on to say that he who glorifies himself has no merit. He who is proud of himself does not last.

Confucius took up this train of thought and wrote decades later: "The moral person has dignity, but no pride. The ordinary person has pride, but no dignity." The moral person, whom Confucius also calls the 'noble one', is characterized by humanity, empathy and justice – all qualities that are diametrically opposed to the narcissist. Because the three chains, self-idealization, devaluation of other people and lack of self-transcendence are tightly tied. Confucius also states that pride is ordinary, the opposite is extraordinary.

For Buddhism, too, pride is seen as a dangerous bondage that binds man to the ephemeral, deceptive 'samsara' – the painful cycle of being. In Buddhism, breaking out of the fatal cycle takes place on the path of letting go of all proud desires, and through knowledge. This is how salvation, 'Nirvana' is achieved.

All these lessons and warnings have not stopped the inhabitants of the Blue Planet from indulging in narcissism in all its forms.

I hope that the readers agree with my analysis, although it may seem harsh, but I can confirm, it is not exaggerated.

Marta

Ninth alpha-mail to Star Omicron 007
Sent and received

The fifth Hermetic law – the Principle of Polarity – in the biography of Rainer Maria Rilke

"Everything is twofold, everything has its pair of opposites; equal and unequal is the same; opposites are identical in nature, only different in degree; extremes touch; all truths are only half-truths; all contradictions can be reconciled." Kybalion

Rainer Maria Rilke, the gifted poet, stands for the principle of polarity. There is no such thing as good and bad, what matters is the perspective from which you look at a situation. Where there is light, there is also shadow. Good and bad, high and low, small and large always form two opposite poles that cannot exist without each other. This implies that opposites are identical, because they just represent different ways of looking at the same thing.

Rainer Maria Rilke (born 1875, Prague, Austria-Hungary, died 1926, Switzerland) is one of the most important German-language poets of his time. He had an extraordinary great sensitivity to interpersonal closeness and distance. He often had a great longing for closeness. Once he made it, it was soon too much for him. He quickly felt hemmed in and fled back into the distance.

As one of the greatest and world-renowned poets, he was a master of language. Nobody could express the interplay of closeness and distance as aptly as he could in language, images and metaphors. In his personal relationships – especially with women – on one hand he feared intimacy, on the other hand, he feared being abandoned.

In Rilke's relationship, 'Be the first to say goodbye', means that he wanted to avoid the narcissistic insult of being abandoned and instead pushed for active abandonment. He lived by the motto: "Whoever goes first, can no longer be left."

The collection of poems 'Sonnets from Orpheus' are among the most important lyrical works of Rilke, along with the 'Duino Elegies':

> *"Be ahead of all farewells as if they were behind*
> *To you, like the winter that is just leaving.*
> *For among winters is one so endless winter,*
> *that, hibernating, your heart survives it all."*

> *(Sei allem Abschied voran, als wäre er hinter*
> *dir, wie der Winter, der eben geht.*
> *Denn unter Wintern ist einer so endlos Winter,*
> *dass, überwinternd, dein Herz überhaupt übersteht.)*

However, the high vulnerability to narcissistic injuries caused by being abandoned also promoted his fear of commitment. Rilke became more and more isolated and he became a withdrawn hermit, for whom poems and letters were the last bridges to life. Rilke was obsessed with two fears that appear psychologically like two sides of a Janus head: He was very afraid of commitment, and at the same time afraid of being abandoned. He had a proximity-distance conflict. If this conflict remains unresolved in the long term, this often leads to significant relationship problems, or even to the failure of relationships.

In the case of Rilke, this basic conflict showed itself superficially in his inability to maintain romantic relationships. He lived with his wife, the sculptor Clara Westhoff, for only seventeen months. The love affair with the married Lou Andreas-Salomé lasted four years. It was by far the longest love affair in his life. He never lived with most of his later lovers.

The older Rilke got the lonelier he became. When he died of cancer (leukemia) at the age of fifty-one, he had been living like a hermit in his domicile in the Chateau de Muzot for a long time.

It is characteristic of ambivalent feelings that the other side always resonates. With Rilke, this applied to love, but also to death. Death as a radical loss was a major life theme for Rilke.

He believed and evoked 'death in the midst of life'. And he was living toward his own death. His cancer forced him to prepare for death through a long, agonizing ordeal.

Death as the 'most radical loss' occupied Rilke for decades in his short life. Deaths from illnesses, suicides and the numerous deaths in the First World War kept him occupied. His cipher of 'death in the midst of life' made death a constant companion for him.

During his first longer trips to Paris in 1902 and 1903, Rilke dealt intensively with the 'mass extinction' in the big city. He immortalized his experiences in his only novel, 'The Notes of Malte Laurids Brigge'.

In this work, a diary novel with which he also showed German prose new paths, it says: "He was a poet and hated the vague." However, there is no lack of dark whispering in Rilke's verses.

There are also brief formulations in his work, which owe their persuasiveness to a wonderful clarity, an astonishing simplicity. Quite a few of these formulations, as plausible as they are memorable and are so easy to quote as Schiller's 'winged words'.

The handy quotations have contributed a great deal to Rilke's popularity – they have helped his work to achieve inconsiderable permanence. One loves the solemn opening of the poem: 'Lord, it is time. The summer was very big'. (Herr, es ist Zeit. Der Sommer war sehr groß.) The atmospheric, elegiac reference is often and happily quoted: "Whoever doesn't have a house now will not build one anymore." (Wer jetzt kein Haus hat, baut sich keines mehr.) And then the difficult to explain magic of the line of the poem: 'And now and then a white elephant'. (Und dann und wann ein weißer Elefant.)

Rilke describes 'The Notes of Malte Laurids Brigge' as a 'book of prose'. This novel was published in two volumes in 1910 and is now regarded as the first modern novel in German literature. In seventy-one notes he describes in the first person the needs, but also a certain maturation process of the penniless Dane Malte, who lives in Paris, and traces his path of increasing loneliness in fragments.

These are shocking experiences of Parisian city life, which for Malte/Rilke consisted of sensory overload, violence, illness, poverty, fear and death. With these stories, Rilke succeeded in coming to terms with his childhood, literature and in recreating his identity.

The notes begin abruptly and laconically on a September afternoon in turn-of-the-century Paris. "11. September, rue Toullier. Well, well, people come here to live, I would rather think it dies here."(11. September, Rue Toullier. So, also hierher kommen die Leute, um zu leben, ich würde eher meinen, es stürbe sich hier.)

Basically, the notes have three different focal points, namely firstly experiences from Malte's childhood and youth in Denmark, then thoughts and experiences in Paris, and thirdly reflections on events, partly historical, partly fictionalized.

Sensory perceptions are a central motif of the recordings and are addressed from the beginning. The newcomer 'sees' on arrival, then 'hears', then 'learns to see', to enter into a process of creation – 'writing'.

Malte's descriptions of the big city that frightens him comes to life above all through the many smells that cling to Paris and the synesthesia that these smells produce. "It smells of poverty, misery and fear. An alley begins to smell. Schoolchildren endure in chambers full of grey-smelling cold. Mama smells ... we all have to be quiet, she smells with her ears, but she stood there with raised eyebrows, attentive and all nose."

(Es riecht nach Armut, Elend und Angst. Eine Gasse beginnt zu riechen. Schulkinder harren aus in Kammern voll grauriechender Kälte. Mama riecht ... da müssen wir immer alle still sein, sie riecht mit den Ohren, dabei aber stand sie selbst mit hochgezogenen Augenbrauen, aufmerksam und ganz Nase.)

Dealing with the phenomenon of the big city is another central motif, as a threatening being that initially takes in the refugees, but then confuses and destroys them with the abundance and hopelessness of life events.

An early poem by Rilke, distributed in millions of copies, made him famous like no other. It is the unforgettable 'Song of

Love and Death by Cornet Christoph Rilke'. (Die Weise von Liebe und Tod des Cornets Christoph Rilke.) One cannot forget this opening: "Ride, ride, ride, through the day, through the night, through the day ... And the courage has grown so tired and the longing so great." (Reiten, reiten, reiten, durch den Tag, durch die Nacht, durch den Tag ... Und der Mut ist so müde geworden und die Sehnsucht so groß.) And then the last line: "There he has seen an old woman cry." (Dort hat er eine alte Frau weinen sehen.)

Rilke's beguiling word music should not be overlooked that he was able to recognize the 'Zeitgeist' very well. He wrote the frequently quoted verse that expresses the suffering of an entire generation: "Who speaks of victories? Survival is everything."(Wer spricht von Siegen? Überstehen ist alles.)

The First World War and the Spanish flu in 1918/1919 confronted him with further collective death threats and deaths. The current corona pandemic makes this situation very topical again: Many changes in social life, the scenarios of 1919 and 2019 show many similarities. The contemporary preventive strategy: keep distance, hygiene/protective masks, rely on heteronomy (vaccination, quarantine, etc.)

"Rilke was the idol of entire generations of German, and even more so, European readers. He was regarded as the embodiment of poetics, his sonorous, rhythmic name – Rainer Maria Rilke – (which fascinates even the Chinese because of the combination of male and female elements) – became the epitome of the poetic. Rilke was a brilliant artist. He knew how to use rhyme like few poets. He has extracted unexpected sounds and melodies from language. In many verses he was able to express what seemed inexpressible. His poetry is a triumph over the unspeakable." This is how the literary critic Marcel Reich-Ranicki describes the lyrical work of Rilke.

'Der Panther: In the Jardin des Plantes, Paris', is considered to be Rilke's most famous 'Ding' poem, in which the poet becomes the speaker of 'dumb things'. During his time in Paris, Rilke was inspired to write the poem due to the sculpture of a panther by Rodin. In this sculpture, the artist Rodin tried to express the essence of a living being.

The panther is considered a symbol of pagan culture, of which the cult of Dionysus was the most representative. He not only belongs to the entourage of the god of intoxication Dionysus, but also to the goddess of love Aphrodite and the sorceress Circe. According to ancient testimonies, he thirsts for wine and needs human excrements to protect himself from being poisoned with aconite.

Shortly after Rodin met the young Rilke, he gave him the advice to go to the Paris Zoo to learn to see properly. Consequently, the animal-loving poet spent a lot of time in the 'Jardin des Plantes' over the next few years. Thus Rilke found in his poem the expression of the insidious stride intensified to the highest point, the mighty striking down of the broad paws, and at the same time the caution in which all strength is wrapped.

The panther is described in three stanzas from its outer appearance – look, gait, eye – in order to open up its interior. In this poem, Rilke solves the problem of the relationship between inside and outside in a very unique way and thus exerts an incredible fascination.

The first stanza begins with the 'look' of the panther, this eye-metaphor describes the relationship to the outside world. Furthermore, the insurmountable limit is marked by the bars of the cage: "He feels as if there were a thousand bars / and behind a thousand bars no world."(Ihm ist, als ob es tausend Stäbe gäbe/ und hinter tausend Stäbe keine Welt.). This repetition of words and sounds makes the desolate situation of the panther clear.

The first quatrain thus describes the tired look, the animal cannot make contact with the world. The deprivation of freedom is expressed through the sluggish rhythm. It is already clear here that the outside world no longer exists for the panther. He is detached from this and is in his own cosmos.

In the second stanza, the form of movement of the panther is described: "The soft gait of supple, strong steps" (Der weiche Gang geschmeidig starker Schritte). Here the contrast of the adjectives, the polarity, 'soft' and 'strong' is particularly striking. He spins in 'the smallest of circles', which is uncharacteristic of captive predators, usually moving right along the edge of the grid. It shows the inner captivity of the panther. The predator has lost its natural character. He's alienated from himself. This is shown by the panther's compulsion to always walk in circles and thus to fill his cosmos with steps.

While the first two stanzas describe the animal from the outside, the third and last line of verse shows the inside of the animal, which perceives its environment in a completely passive manner. It confirms the outer and inner captivity. But then a moment is described in which the circular steps of the panther suddenly stop. An image of the outside world comes through his eyes straight into his heart.

At the center of this poem is a 'thing' that acquires a symbolic meaning. The poet identifies himself in the panther. The sense of imprisonment was intended to match Rilke's sense of loneliness in Paris. He feels like he's the panther. Due to the limitation of its perception, the predator can no longer act actively, the interaction between environment and action is destroyed, and with it the living being itself, which only exists as a whole in this interaction. The panther represents man in the tension between life and death.

Rainer Maria Rilke lived the condition of the genius. This made his life so lonely.

Lotus

Tenth alpha-mail to Star Omicron 007
    Sent and received

The sixth Hermetic law – the Principle of Cause and Effect – in the biography of Agatha Christie

"For every action there is a reaction. Nothing happens without a reason. Every effect has its cause, everything happens according to law. All processes of life are connected to each other. Coincidence is but the name of an unknown law." Kybalion

Agatha Christie was born in Torquay, Devon, in 1890, the youngest child of an American father and an English mother. She was not taught at school until she was sixteen years old, but by her mother, who recognized her talent as a writer at an early age.

Agatha Miller gave up her music studies in Paris at the beginning of the First World War, and worked as a nurse (Voluntary Aid Detachment) with the British Red Cross in a hospital, subsequently in a pharmacy. During this time she gained a lot of experience about poisons and their effects, which later played a role in her works.

In 1914 she married Colonel Archibald Christie, an aviator in the Royal Air Force. With him she had one daughter, Rosalind Margaret Clarissa, who was born in the year 1919.

Her first crime novel, 'The Mysterious Affair at Styles', starring the Belgian detective Hercule Poirot (first kept as a hairdresser by strangers because of his magnificent mustache), was published in 1920, first in the United States and later in England. Christie became suddenly famous with the work 'Alibi' (The Murder of Roger Ackroyd), published in 1926.

This is considered a highly accomplished work, but one that sparked widespread controversy even among Christie's fans. Because at the end of the novel, contrary to previous conventions, it turns out that the novel's first-person narrator is the murderer, who initially had something like a trust bonus among the readership.

Privately, the 1920s were rather unfortunate for Christie. Her husband often left her alone for work reasons, and her mother died in 1926 – an event that affected her greatly. In the same year, her husband confessed of having an affair with his golf partner. Despite attempts of reconciliation, the couple fell apart more and more. After a heated argument on December 3rd of the same year, Agatha Christie left the house. Her car was found abandoned by a lake a few days later. The police search report showed a photo of the missing person and read:

"MISSING Mrs. Agatha Mary Clarissa Christie, wife of Colonel A. Christie. Age 35 years, height 5ft'7, hair color red (short), natural teeth, gray eyes, fair complexion, well built … Left home in a four seater Morris Cowley at 09:45 evening 3rd December.

Left a note saying she'll be taking a trip by wagon … If you have seen this woman or have any information as to her whereabouts, report to any police station or to Charles Goddard, Wokingham Station Chief directly."

After a spectacular search operation, which was also reported by the New York Times and in which Sir Arthur Conan Doyle (the inventor of Sherlock Holmes) was involved, Agatha Christie was found ten days after her disappearance in a hotel in Harrogate, where she had been staying under the name of her husband's mistress.

As a result, the British Parliament also dealt with the cost of the search operation. Her family circulated the story that she had almost total memory loss for those days. Agatha Christie herself never revealed her motives, not even in her memoirs. In 1928 her marriage to Archibald Christie ended in divorce. As Agatha Christie remarked, "Love should be a joyful feeling – not something that hurts so terribly."

In order to recover from the losses and catastrophes of the past few years, she decided relatively spontaneously to make repeated trips to the Middle East. This quick decision was to change Agatha Christie's life significantly and exert a great influence on her literary work.

During her second stay in Ur, she met the archaeologist Max Mallowan, who was fourteen years her junior, and the two fell in love. Agatha Christie reluctantly accepted Mallowan's proposal and they were married in Edinburgh in 1930. One of her well-known quotes in this context: "An archaeologist is the best husband a woman can have: the older she gets, the more interesting she becomes to him."

In the same year of her marriage, a new detective made his debut in the novel 'The Murder at the Vicarage': the spinster Miss Marple (she always insists to be addressed Miss), who also appears in twelve other crime novels, takes the lead.

This elderly lady of 74 is a non-technical lead detective whose main weapon, in solving crimes, is seemingly insignificant small talk. Like Poirot, she's a grown character, she works because of her affectionate quirks, however he works for very different reasons. Both personalities are not stereotypical investigators. Her killer characters are mostly desperate, broken figures, but she draws them with sympathy. Christie took this to the extreme in 'Murder on the Orient Express', and represents an essential contrast, by even justifying the murder.

Christie wrote many of the numerous novels produced in the years leading up to 1958 during archaeological expeditions with her husband in northern Iraq and Syria. A number of her novels are also set in the Middle East, for example 'They Came to Baghdad' or 'Murder in Mesopotamia'.

Marked by the life-threatening event following the separation and divorce from her first husband, Christie wrote two crime novels in the 1940s, which she held back for later publication. 'Curtain', Hercule Poirot's last case, prepared her for publication when it became apparent that she would not write another novel. The work was published shortly before her death and it is indeed Poirot's last case, as he dies at the end of the investigation.

Hercule Poirot was Christie's main source of income, and it was necessary for him to solve a few more cases before 'Curtain' came out. 'Sleeping murder', starring Miss Marpel as the detective, was the second novel Christie held back and was published after her death in 1976, at the age of 85.

With Hercule Poirot, Agatha Christie invented an unprecedented type of investigator. This retired senior Belgian official was very un-English in appearance and demeanor and usually conducted his investigations among the British upper class. This was a conscious trick of her, since one of the fundamental problems in crime novels of the 19th and early 20th centuries was the detective's social class. Police officers tended to come from the lower social classes. In Great Britain, where class barriers were still in place after the end of the Second World War, it would have been inconceivable that a member of the 'lower' class would, or could easily investigate 'upper' class'.

With Poirot as the protagonist, Christie has devised an elegant and original workaround. Because he is an outsider, due to his origin, for whom the high British class barriers do not apply. The characterful detective figure seems almost made to provide the reader with clues to identify the perpetrators in the novels, but at the same time to lure them down the wrong track (red herrings).

As a writer, Christie demonstrated a generally sensitive sociological sense of class differences, for example in 'Death on the Nile' she tells of worlds about to collide, of colonialism in Africa, of the self-confident American culture in conflict with the European culture, shattered by the First World War, and often by very different images of women.

On board the Nile steamer Karnak, a self-assured, half-American heiress collides with a fellow passenger caught in the conventions of class society. The political horizon of the time is also mentioned, for example when a fervent Marxist gets into discussions at the scene of the action.

She has perfected the claustrophobic chamber play as an image of human abysses. Exotic locations only serve as a backdrop. Nothing is more frightening than the closed space. It's petty crimes that grow out of private tragedies, it's the ordinary that makes the killer, not the extraordinary that drives the serial killers who later become rampant in crime novels.

Agatha Christie was a 24/7 writer who drew inspiration for her characters or entire plots from many everyday things. From the moment she came up with ideas, she demonstrated qualities as a tireless worker. She was constantly making notes and working on and with them. She not only wrote down ideas, but also made lists for characters, motives, types of murder or locations. She often evaluated old notebooks again and drew from her rich fundus.

Christie tried not to repeat herself and showed a talent for variations. The different perspectives of the novels in the authorial, personal or first-person narrative situation show a love of experimentation. Despite high productivity, she didn't want to let boredom arise.

She also had humor and sarcasm, as evidenced by some of her quotes. "Since Lucrezia Borgia, I've been the woman who has killed the most people, albeit with a typewriter." She also had an aversion to journalists, who, like her, earned their money by writing. "I've never liked journalists. I let them all die in my books." Or: "If you want to be a lovely lady at seventy, you have to start as a 17-year-old girl." "Men are all the same: easy to catch with flattery and a pretty mask."

The writer liked to live very nicely and comfortably, but she didn't think much of housework: "I'm not going to run around doing amateurish things that someone else does for a small sum with professional skill."

What makes her works extraordinary is that the author, like no other, runs the unraveling game with tremendous bustle on all three levels, as a perpetrator riddle, a riddle of the course of events and an unveiling riddle. From the outset, the fact that Christie locates her puzzling fun in most of her stories in social circles of the 'gentry' appears to be a trick. The background for this is less about the representation of an 'ideal world'. The stratum of society, the vaguely defined upper middle class and lower nobility, provided a useful background for Christie's expansion and complication of the puzzle structure.

Conveniently, social contacts between members of this class are usually limited to the formal and superficial. Since they often hide their true colors behind a mask, so to speak, the plausibility of the story in this milieu remains intact for the readership, despite all of Christie's game of concealment in order to entertain.

In addition to her writing activities, Christie supported her second husband, the archaeologist, in his excavations, particularly in the restoration of prehistoric ceramics (which she cleaned with her own skin creams), and the photo documentation of the finds. One of her humorous remarks: "Shards bring luck – but only to the archaeologist." She contributed significantly to the financing of his expeditions.

In 1971, Agatha Christie was inducted into the Order of the British Empire as a 'Dame Commander' by Queen Elizabeth II. and thereby raised to personal nobility.

Christie wrote a total of sixty-six crime novels, short stories and stage works, which have also been filmed several times with great success for cinema and television, and adapted for the stage. She also made a career in theater, because after having bad experiences, she decided to adapt her plays for the stage herself and was enthusiastically involved in the production. One of her plays was 'The Mousetrap', which was the longest running play in the world.

The world's best-selling detective novel 'And Then There Were None' (originally titled: 'Ten Little Niggers', borrowed from a well-known children's song) was written with consideration and published to the American readers in a way that is in line with the market.

Current estimates, according to the heirs and publishers, assume a total sold circulation of over two billion books worldwide. According to UNESCO's Index 'Translationum', she ranks first by a wide margin on the list of the most translated authors. She is considered the most successful crime writer in the world.

Because of this success, she is also called the Queen of Crime. In 2000, she was named 'Best Crime Writer of the Century' at the Anthony Bucher Memorial World Mystery Convention.

Agatha Christie was already a well-known writer when she had the mysterious and dramatic upheaval in her life due to the breakdown of her marriage. However, it was only possible to reach these heights of literary achievement because this woman had to reinvent herself in her pain and despair. Fate has broken a woman here in order to heal her. The cause was the loss of her will to live, and the effect was to become the unique crime writer of the century.

Dame Agatha Christie's mysteries are still entertaining today. I also plan to write such a piece of literature with many 'red herrings'.

To be continued ... Marta

Eleventh alpha-mail to Star Omicron 007
    Sent and received

Narcissism and the Post-Growth Economy

"The world has enough for everyone's needs, but not enough for everyone's greed." This quote from Mahatma Gandhi characterizes the threatening situation of the Blue Planet.

The inhabitants of the Blue Planet have lived and survived for thousands of years without significant economic growth. It was not until industrialization that this process began on a large scale, setting in motion an unprecedented technological and social development. There was a significant improvement in the quality of life for broad sections of the population. Running water, electricity, healthy housing, enough healthy food, education, equal rights, etc. raised the standard of living for millions. Undoubtedly, economic growth initially had positive effects in terms of size and quality.

However, this does not mean that this growth has not had any problematic side effects, such as great social tensions. But in the last half century the negative effects have increased so much that the whole concept has to be questioned. Depletion of non-renewable resources, environmental degradation, climate change, dependence on energy sources of foreign countries, rising sea levels, regional water shortages, extinction of species, war and terror, flight of millions, and other phenomena are cited as evidence that economic growth – as it is now being practiced – could bring about the end of the planet Earth. The big issue is whether economic growth means the demise of the entire planet, or on the contrary, it is the only solution – in a modified form – of the current crises of the world community.

Only profit-oriented industrialization, turbo-capitalism, neoliberalism, etc. are symptoms of a disturbed socio-cultural development. Humans are only misused as an instrument for maximizing profits and downgraded to 'homo consumens'.

Both, the Covid-19 crisis and the current war conflict between Ukraine and Russia, are affecting a society that has been ill for some time. There is no end in sight to these catastrophes. hundred of thousands of people are dying in this process: Ukraine must not lose, the Russians cannot win. According to Neumann's game theory, a 'lose-lose' situation has arisen in which each participant can only lose.

What possibilities do different schools of thought have to divert the destructive path of growth? A 'culture of enough' is needed. The current major crises of the Blue Planet can only be solved with a 'satisfied frugality'. Sociological research has amply demonstrated that accumulating material goods of the same kind do not make man happier. The 'homo ludens' does not have enough time available to play with all his technical instruments and gadgets – always the latest model. There is no longer a need for constant renewal.

Sufficiency means self-limitation of human demands. The 'earthlings' see themselves exclusively as beneficiaries of rights and freedoms. Like many narcissists, they do not accept any duties and responsibilities for themselves. On a personal level, the narcissists predominantly harm their partners within the same timeline. The economic decisions, on the other hand, deprive the grandchildren and great-grandchildren of any healthy livelihood.

In the last few decades, a level of material demands has emerged that does not make people happier and that the planet cannot meet. "We have become a society of I, I, I" – says the economist and Nobel Prize winner Paul A. Samuelson, referring to the energies that many people – especially narcissists – bring to the shaping of their everyday lives. An oversupply of goods and services, the omnipresence of the media, aggressive advertising and an ever increasing gap between rich and poor make it difficult to find a way out of this vicious circle. But things can't go on like this. And there is no going back to the good old days, which never existed.

In the discussion about global crises, one term is omnipresent: the 'Anthropocene': climate change, radioactive waste, microplastics – the list of consequences of human actions is so long that it has been proposed to name an entire geological era after humans. The human factor always plays an important role in economic activities: capital investments in China have led to a large leap in growth, while in Africa capital flows have produced little.

Necessity not only has negative aspects, necessity also makes people inventive, opens up new possibilities and seeks solutions outside of one's own nose. It is reported that Seve Ballesteros only had a 3-iron when he started playing golf as a caddy. And that had been given to him because it wasn't perfect anymore. And Seve used that single golf club for the drive, for the fairway, for the shot from the sand, and for putting on the green. And every golfer knows what heights this golfer took his game to by overcoming the most incredible obstacles early in his career.

In a famous parable, 'Heaven and Hell', both situations are presented in the same image. A group of people are seated around a table on which is a large cauldron of steaming soup. Everyone is hungry, and they stay hungry in hell, because the spoons have such long handles that they can't eat, they can only feed the neighbors. In heaven, everyone gets fed and is happy with this kind, yet wise method.

The author of this parable is Rabbi Haim, who lived in Turkey in the first half of the 19th century and passed on many other wisdoms to his students. It's frightening when you consider that the food waste alone from the Western World – that which hasn't spoiled – would be enough to feed all the children of the Third World. Greed makes a humane distribution impossible, because there is no profit to be made from it.

In the early 1970's there was an international situation that would have allowed the petrodollars of the oil-exporting countries to be invested in the Third World with the help of the technological know-how of Western countries. Regional and national development banks should bring the three parties together in 'Trilateral Cooperation'. The overly long spoons – the greed of all three parties – has let this development potential fizzle out for the whole world. (Trilateral Cooperation, Traute Scharf, OECD, Paris, 1978.)

Growth is the most important basis for the functioning of the market economy. To describe the pursuit of material possessions as 'greedy' is no exaggeration. Therefore, the term 'greed economy' is certainly not inappropriate in the current situation. This 'greed economy' obtains stability from a supposed 'win-win' situation. In feedback, the maximization system drives people more and more to live out their longing for property, status, long-distance travel and illusions more drastically. All of these parameters fit the profile of narcissism.

This desire to consume more and more leads people to buy things they don't need, with the money they don't have, in order to impress people they don't care about. A consumption that one cannot actually afford is the pledging of the future that has become a matter of course – with immense debt repayment and supply obligations. This points to the pressure exerted by the 'greed economy'.

This wish for always more consumer goods and services is neither sustainable nor viable. It is defined by expansion and permanent growth. Without these principles it would collapse. This system is being defended by all means, as activities during the 2008 financial crisis clearly demonstrated. It is not the human striving for growth that is reprehensible, but the exclusive striving for gain and profit as the sole motivating factors.

The limitations of the Blue Planet and its resources doom the pure growth economy to fail. In order for this not to be a 'crash', but rather a 'turning point by design', man must, in his own interest, put narcissistic characteristics such as self-interest, consumerism and excess on the back burner.

The people of the Blue Planet are currently living in a permanent flood. No low tide far and wide. A flood of consumer goods, services, information, countless opportunities to participate in events and travel. It takes strength to stand against this tide in order not to be swept away.

Not only the climate warms up drastically. Heated debates and heated tempers make all living beings suffer. The media also contribute to the unfavorable warming of social coexistence. Events and developments are literally shouted out. The business with the news is overturning.

How refreshing is an aphorism from the mystic Angelus Silesius: "A fool tries a lot, all the doing of the wise. / That is ten times nobler, is love, look, rest." ('Ein Narr ist viel bemüht, des Weisen ganzes Tun/ das zehnmal edler, ist Lieben, Schauen, Ruhn') The 'earthlings' only have this one planet. A 'turning point by design' is definitely preferable to a 'big crash'.

An eminent theologian and Jesuit, Karl Rahner, proclaimed that the Christian and man of the 21st century will be 'mystical', or will not be. (Writings on theology, VII, 22f.) In principle, this means nothing other than that the people on the Blue Planet must learn to act and live according to Hermetic Principles, or they will perish.

Rahner's view and analysis from the 1960s has lost nothing of its importance, and some things have probably become more acute. Globalization currently exists through technology, media and the market. The radical transformation process can no longer be steered. The inhabitants of the Blue Planet experience the breaking of traditions in the great human experiment.

Karl Rahner's often quoted statement that the human being of the 21st century will be a 'mystic', means also that mankind has to live a new spirituality that is based on a strongly personal choice of freedom. Courage for good contradiction and profiled pluralism is also required, against a time that tends more and more towards totalitarianism and the dominance of just one point of view. The spirituality of the future will be directed against the idols of wealth, pleasure and uncontrolled power – against narcissism!

The current situation on the Blue Planet is marked by a radical ambivalence. The 'earthling' is now in danger of destroying himself. Not so much with conscious intention, but because of the inner consequences of the dynamic. On the one hand, there is the inner limitlessness of self-manipulated actions (nuclear fission, gene manipulation, etc.). On the other hand, it is the inner baselessness of the use of power, as shown by totalitarian structures.

One of the dumbest proverbs on the Blue Planet is: 'One learns from damage'. Mankind surpasses itself in its inability to learn from damage, as the ubiquitous armed conflicts alone prove.

Throughout human history there has always been scarcity. Scarcity was a constant: not enough food, not enough water, not enough security, not enough medical care, etc. While consumption used to mean liberation from a state of need, today consumption has become a sign of identity, from designer clothes to watches, cars, smartphones, etc.

In the past, only a small part of the population could afford excessive consumption, the nobility and the clergy. Today, in the Western World, a much larger percentage indulge in consumption that exceeds human limits. Planet Earth has only finite resources, but people live and work as if there could never be a shortage. The generations of the future are completely sacrificed to narcissistic thinking and acting.

It is not yet clear how a postgrowth economy for eight billion people would work. There is still no 'Model B' on a global scale. However, there are national and regional attempts to consider factors other than economic parameters.

A country in Asia is trying with remarkable success to put economic development behind the factors of environmental protection, climate neutrality, sensible use of natural resources, controlled tourism, social justice, etc.

That country is Bhutan, a small State between the great powers of China to the north and India to the south. Bhutan is also called the land of the thunder dragon, Drukpa-Yul, land of the happiest people. The dragon is on the national flag, red for royalty, and yellow for Buddhism.

This religion and philosophy has much in common with the Hermetic principles. As the Dalai Lama wrote: 'Ethics are more important than religions'. With every economic action, the motivation has to be questioned and this human factor is decisive for a positive effect of economic actions.

The present king's father, affectionately known as K4, who was the fourth king of the dynasty, introduced 'Gross National Happiness', at the end of the 1970's. This is a diverse parameter for the general development of the country, unique in the whole world.

Bhutan is a poor country by western standards. International development aid was also provided in this way. The king wished for schools for the young people in the great heights of the Himalayas and hospitals for all his subjects. Education and medical care are provided freely for all national residents of Bhutan.

Whenever a project was completed, the king's acknowledgment was famous: "Thank you for the school, this is my palace. Thank you for the hospital, that's my palace too." This attitude is diametrically opposed to any narcissism, that practices a pure 'greed economy' – profit, growth, competition – not only in economic matters.

The first mention of the term 'Gross National Happiness', and thus also the coining of the term, happened in 1979. In an interview with an Indian journalist, the king was asked how high the Gross National Product (GNP) of his country was.

Instead of answering, the king replied that in Bhutan 'Gross National Happiness' is more important than GNP. This first mention of a term represented a spontaneous reaction from the king. It was more than a play of words, it was an holistic and overarching concept.

The king invented a descriptive term for striving for economic development that also does justice to Bhutan's culture and values. It goes beyond the concept of man as 'homo oeconomicus', defined only as producer and consumer. A ministry for 'Happiness and Well-being' watches over this, which randomly checks the condition of the population every five years.

Besides Bhutan, which as a whole country is a laboratory for a 'Model B' growth economy, there are also five blue zones on the Blue Planet, home of the healthiest and longest-living populations, none of which indulge in limitless economic growth.

Blue zones are not the richest areas in the world. In fact, the lives of these people are marked by remarkable simplicity. These areas are sporadically scattered across the planet Earth. This means that they all have different choices of production and food.

In all blue zones, people eat mainly plant-based and local products. They are never overweight, never eat to their fullest. 'Hara hachi bu' is their motto. Translations are often difficult, the faithful are not beautiful, the beautiful are not faithful. But there is still room for complication. 'Belly needle book' is the literal translation. 'Eating only up to 80% of saturation', is an elegant analogous variant. Vulgo: 'Don't eat until you burst'.

The blue zones include the Japanese island of Okinawa, also known as the island of the immortals. On the Nicoya Peninsula in Costa Rica, a 'plan de vida', a meaning of life, is also held to be important. The Banbaya region, island of the centenarians in Sicily, and the green island of Ikaria also belong to these lucky areas.

Loma Linda is the only blue zone that is not geographically isolated. It is a small town in California, populated primarily by 'Seven-day Adventists', a Protestant-Baptist church. These people are very religious, abstain entirely from alcohol and drugs and do a lot of physical work. They live ten years longer than the average American.

Residents of all blue zones spend a lot of time outdoors. They are exposed to plenty of fresh air and sunlight on a daily basis. This ensures the production of vitamin D and, as a result, a generally good mood. And this way of life protects these people from diseases of civilization – which plague many narcissists – and does not cost a lucrative penny.

In all these areas people have a conscious goal. The Okinawans call it 'Ikigai'. Roughly speaking, this means: 'Why I get up in the morning.' In all of these different societies, connection with family, village, community and nature is a major concern. They extract no more from the soil than is needed. They do not pollute the air with industrial emissions of carbon dioxide, which is responsible for the greenhouse effect and global warming. There is no growth frenzy there. Permanent sales increase, profit maximization, expansion – are not even foreign words for these people. Narcissists have no chance of success in the blue zones. Nobody plays with them.

Dear Gowinda!

As a summary I send you a song: Just as the Beatles sang half a century ago: 'All you need is love', today's hit is: 'All you need is less'. This is also the title of a book: Niko Paech, et al., 2020.

I hope you like the melody.

As always,
  your Lotus

Twelfth Alpha Mail to Star Omicron 007
  Sent and received

The seventh Hermetic Law – the Principle of Gender – in the biography of Hildegard von Bingen

"Gender is in everything, everything has male and female principles, gender is revealed on all levels." Kybalion.

Hildegard von Bingen stands for the principle of gender, which can only unfold its full effect in connection with both forces of the sex. No other woman in the Middle Ages combined female and male characteristics so well and used them for the good of the people.

Among other things, she expresses her concise aphorisms and striking wisdom: "Man has more creative power than woman. But woman is a fountain of wisdom and abundance of joy. The man brings both to perfection." And more of her sayings: "Many men, if they remain without women, are as inglorious as a day without sun. Without the woman, the man could not be called man, without the man, the woman could not be called woman."

Hildegard lived from 1098 to 1179 in Germany on the banks of the Rhine, she came from a noble family. Her occupation is given as a Benedictine abbess, doctor, poet, composer and natural healing polymath. Another source gives only a laconic description of her profession: a saint.

The name Hildegard means 'heroine', or rather 'rescuing one, shielding hero maiden'. She was born in the dynamic period of the European High Middle Ages. This was the time of the Crusades, intellectual innovations, growing economy and society, new developments in religion, science, literature and art.

Already at the age of three, Hildegard is said to have had visionary talent. She later calls this power of vision the 'living light' and says: "During my first formation, when God awakened me in my mother's womb with the breath of life, he impressed this vision on my soul."

Hildegard von Bingen is considered the first female representative of German mysticism in the Middle Ages, a vocation previously reserved for men only. Her works deal with religion, medicine, ethics and cosmology. She was also an advisor to many high personalities. An extensive correspondence from her has been preserved, which also contains clear admonitions towards high-ranking male contemporaries, including Emperor Friedrich I. – Barbarossa.

This emperor was admired by his contemporaries as the restorer of the empire and the embodiment of chivalric ideals. Hildegard steadfastly admonished this mighty one: "May the Holy Spirit teach you to live and work according to His righteousness."

Hildegard grew up on her father's manor house and, as her parent's tenth child. At the age of eight, she was placed in a Benedictine monastery as an oblate in religious education (a tents to God). That was the custom of the high nobility at the time. For generations, monasteries have been the recognized centers of classical education and science, which explains their great appeal.

Hildegard was placed in the care of a relative, Jutta von Spannheim, who had settled with other women in a hermitage near the Benedictine Abbey on the Disibodenberg. The typical rhythm of life, according to the rule of St. Benedict of Nursia, shaped the days. According to the season, there was a prayer period of four to eight hours a day, and seven to eight hours of sleep. The rest of the time was divided equally between work, religious reading and study.

Hildegard learned to read, write, Latin, sing psalms and various liberal arts in the monastic three-step process of 'lectio', 'meditatio' and 'oratio', alternating between study, meditation and prayer. At the age of fifteen she entered the order. She was considered an outstanding personality who had extensive biblical, theological, philosophical and natural history knowledge. So Hildegard's life as a nun took place over decades in the simple Benedictine balance.

In 1136 Hildegard was elected 'Magistra' of the assembled nun students. There were several arguments with the abbot, because Hildegard moderated asceticism, one of the principles of monasticism, and she was against ascetic punishment and wearing penitential belts, thus demonstrating her philanthropy. So she relaxed the dietary regulations in her community and shortened the very long prayer and service times.

She also advocated drinking beer: "Cerevisiam bibat!" Drink beer for health. Everyone who was ignorant of Latin probably understood this. By the way, the alcohol content of beer in the 12th century was much lower than today. It should also not be forgotten that at that time coffee, black and green tea as well as cocoa were still unknown in Europe.

Open dispute broke out when Hildegard wanted to found her own monastery with her community. The Benedictines of Disibodenberg, near Bingen, strongly opposed this, since Hildegard brought popularity and income to their monastery.

Against the will of the abbot, she left her monastery at the age of fifty to build her own monastery on the Ruprechtsberg in Bingerbrück, where the river Nahe flows into the Rhine. According to her plans, with the help of two hundred Cistercian monks, a huge monastery complex was built within two years, which was admired and marveled at by her contemporaries: "Has something like this ever been seen? A woman builds her own monastery without the support of church and state!" – She also fought for the economic independence of her newly founded monastery, demonstrating not only her organizational skills but also her business acumen.

At the age of sixty-five, Hildegard acquired the Eibingen monastery on the other side of the Rhine near Rüdesheim, where she accommodated non-noble women who wanted to live in her community. Even in old age she seems to be very vigorous, she rowed twice a week from Bingerbrück through the torrent river to look after her fellow sisters.

Hildegard's enthusiasm for work knows no bounds. At the age of seventy she still gets on her horse to ride and preach throughout Germany. With great enthusiasm she mingles with the people to spread her message.

At the age of eighty she is still fighting like an Antigone against her church administration, which demands that she dig up an excommunicated knight in her monastery cemetery. She is punished with an interdict, she is no longer allowed to sing her songs, and the church doors are bricked up. She fights for her rehabilitation for a whole year and wins. The ban on the church is lifted.

At the end of her life, Hildegard confesses in her vita: "As long as I work on my visionary work, I don't feel like an old woman, but like a young girl!"

To justify her written texts, Hildegard referred to visions that, according to her own account, became irresistibly powerful in 1141. This is how she hears the inner command: "Write down what you see, and say what you hear."

Hildegard von Bingen was a great healer like the 'herbal women' of the early Celtic and Germanic times. Since her healing successes often could not be explained rationally, they were regarded as a kind of miracle. Since Hildegard was both a prophetess of the Word of God and an abbess, her healing work was considered divine miracle.

Without this background, she would probably have been branded as a witch, like so many successful healers over the centuries. The worst effects of this condemnation of inexplicable healing were later punished in the witch trials of the Inquisition. Perhaps this approach by the church is one of the reasons why Hildegard's merits have been forgotten for so long.

Her books are themed on the Word of Christ: Know the ways (Scivias), the truth (On the values of life), and the divine life (Of the divine works). In addition, she adheres to the rule of the Benedictines to connect the earthly with the heavenly. "A truly holy person welcomes all that is earthly."

Her main work 'Scivias' was written over a period of ten years. This book is a doctrine in which the worldview and the human image are inseparably interwoven with the image of God. This faith consists of three parts and spans the arc from the creation of the world and man to the coming into being, and as well as the development of the church to the redemption and perfection of the world at the end of times.

Hildegard works on it for many arduous years. In the end, 'Scivias' is one of the most impressive world panoramas of the Middle Ages, from which Pope Eugene III., during the reform synod in Trier, 1147, read to the bishops assembled there. A process that was unthinkable until then. Now the content of Hildegard's writing was confirmed and her 'visio' certified by the highest ecclesiastical authority.

Pope Eugene III. had placed Hildegard in a sensational way in the world public. He had awarded Hildegard's work the title 'Out of God's Wisdom'. Everyone of rank and fame makes a pilgrimage to her for advice. The Disibodenberg becomes the consulting room of Europe, emperors and kings, popes and prince-bishops, but also the common people seek advice from Hildegard.

The second visionary work 'Liber vitae meritorum' (Book of Life's Merits) could be described as visionary ethics. Thirty-five vices and virtues are contrasted. On the way to a happy and meaningful life, every person should deal with their mistakes and strengths, the virtues and vices that either promote or block their life. The path to healing is to transform the thirty-five destructive forces of the soul into positive ones. Here in lies the key to a life full of love, zest for life and health.

The third book 'Liber divinorum operum' (Book of Divine Works) is Hildegard's view of the world and man, the origin of the universe, the processes of creation and the role that man plays in the universe.

During the Synod in Trier, Hildegard received in the year 1147 from Pope Eugene III. permission to publish her visions. The Pope wrote about the 'prophetissa teutonica', the German prophetess: "You have become a scent of life for many."

This recognition also strengthened her political importance. Her self-confident and charismatic demeanor made her famous. She was the first nun to publicly preach conversion to God to the people, on preaching trips to Mainz, Würzburg, Bamberg, Trier, Metz, Bonn and Cologne.

Her extensive correspondence with high ecclesiastical (including Bernhard von Clairvaux) and secular dignitaries, which has been preserved in around three hundred documents, is also part of her theological oeuvre. In it she shows her extraordinarily strong character and faith in God. For her time, her open words and admonitions, which she used against the emperor, and prince bishops, were particularly remarkable. In that sense, she was also an influential politician.

Between the years 1150 and 1160, Hildegard wrote two natural and medicinal works. So she became the first writing doctor. All thirteen textual witnesses were written down a hundred years after her death, or even later, so that her authorship was partly doubted. However, in the works undoubtedly attributed to her, a treatise on natural history entitled 'The Book of the Mysteries of the Various Natures of Creatures', is mentioned.

This could mean the great work on the properties and effects of herbs, trees, precious stones, animals and metals, which was later printed under the name 'Physia': "With the help of nature, mankind can create everything that is necessary and life-sustaining. Humanity finds itself in the middle of the world. Amidst all creatures, humanity is the most remarkable, but also the most dependent on others."

Hildegard continues: "The Earth should not be injured. The Earth shall not be destroyed. Whenever the elements of the world are profaned by ill treatment, God will cleanse them through the suffering and distress of mankind."

A second work, called 'Causae et curae' (Causes and Treatments), is a general account of creation, of nature, and of human nature in particular. Hildegard's achievements lie, among other things, in the fact that she brought together the knowledge of the time about diseases and plants from the Greek-Latin tradition with that of folk medicine, and used the German plant names.

"Herbs give each other the fragrance of their blossoms. One stone shines its splendor on the other, and everything that lives has a primal urge for a loving embrace ... My heart is overflowing to give help to everyone. I am considerate of all needs. I pick up the infirm and lead them to recovery. I am ointment for every ailment, and my words do good."

Above all, she developed her own views on the origin of diseases, physical and mental. Hildegard's disease theory is very similar to the ancient theory of the four humors, only with different names. "Man's stomach and bladder absorb everything with which he nourishes himself. When these two get too much food and drink, they cause a storm of evil juices throughout the body, like the elements after the manner of man."

The herbalism of 'Causae et curae' contains many direct instructions, each grouped by symptoms. They are therefore also easy to use for medical laypersons. For example, it says: "When a person's hearing is destroyed by some phlegm or other kind of disease, white incense is taken and smoke is emitted from it over living fire and let this smoke rise into the obturated ear ..."

Comparative studies have shown that Hildegard's medicine is unique and original and has not been copied either from the monastic medicine of the time, or from contemporary Arabic medicine.

Hildegard appeals to the personal responsibility of the individual for itself and its body. This also applies to spiritual life. Just as everything that the body absorbs is converted into juices that bring illness or health to the organism, thoughts can also make you satisfied or ill.

The one who faces and fights against his illness is obeying the divine requirement of his mind and character. If he stays calm and confident, he can get his illness under control and bring back the 'verditas'. For Hildegard, this is a term for the 'Green', symbolizing physical and mental health in a healthy being. The heart of her healing art is the right measure in all things – the 'discretio'.

Therefore, her diagnoses are usually followed by preventive recommendations, such as responsible body care and thoughtful eating. The four pillars of Hildegard's medicine are nutrition, remedies, detoxification and fasting. For Hildegard there is no essential difference between illnesses of the mind and of the body. In her opinion, diseases can only be treated effectively if the patient changes his attitude to life.

The term 'Hildegard-medicine' was only introduced as a marketing term in the 1970s. Only after eight hundred years did a worldwide renaissance of Hildegard's medicine began, which is still support and orientation for more and more people today. Hildegard-research has meanwhile gained worldwide importance. In Europe, countless research groups and Hildegard societies deal with her writings and work. In recent years there has been an increased interest from the United States and Asia.

The idea of unity and wholeness is also the key to Hildegard's natural and medicinal work. She writes: "Man has three paths within himself, in which his life is active: the soul, the body and the senses." This is what makes Hildegard's ideas so fascinating, that she enables a view of the whole, that she sees the connections between body and soul, between the different areas and forces of the cosmos. Again and again, she looks at people who are aligned with the macrocosm, which surrounds them in diverse circles and affects them.

Worldwide studies confirm what Hildegard specifically describes, that with a good diet and a sensible lifestyle, the rate of chronic auto-aggression diseases such as heart attacks, strokes, cancer and rheumatism could be reduced by 80 %.

Last but not least, Hildegard's influence is so great and lasting, because she not only lived the cosmic principle of gender, but also made all the other cosmic principles her guidelines.

I'm not so knowledgeable about mysticism, I leave this to my later age. However, I admire Hildegard von Bingen for her male courage, medical knowledge, and the wisdom of the human soul.
Marta

Thirteenth Alpha mail to Star Omicron 007
Sent and received

Homecoming to the Stars

Carissima Gowinda!

I love Italian cuisine and Italian art. Look again at the painting of Narcissus that Caravaggio created. In this artwork, the baroque master anticipated the problems of the 21st century with his brush. And he gave me the idea of a present for you, although it is not visible in his picture. Did I make you curious?

In my mind I'm already on my way home to the Stars – and to you. I will no longer write the 'Back-to-Galaxy' report on the Blue Planet, but during the 'galactic beam' through space. My homesickness is so great and my longing for you infinite.

With my last report on the issues of economic growth – yes or no – I have gathered all the necessary facts for the final mission report. The 'earthlings' have many hidden faculties and qualities, but now they have to develop and use them much more.

The inhabitants of the Blue Planet are like piano players who only strum one octave. However, a piano consists of seven octaves. So they only have mental and roughly sensual abilities, while in depth of consciousness there are potentials to grasp reality in a completely different way.

On the Blue Planet the potential was activated only to the extent necessary for the survival of the species. If the conditions for survival change, then new, unknown potencies must be awakened. In this way, some ethnic groups developed skills thar are not found in the majority of 'earthlings'. For example, among the aborigines of Australia, telepathy was observed; this was necessary for community survival in hunting and warding off danger.

The 'earthlings' seem to ignore their hidden potentials. Yet not only the dogmas of the Roman Catholic Church, but also the paradigms of mankind were developed at a time when the planet Earth was thought to be flat and the stars to be holes in the firmament.

The final report will be a difficult task, but I will not undertake it until I have returned home to our Star. The one-sided and long-term dependence on cheap energy, on the only Russian source, will bring many politicians into a state of emergency that they cannot justify with any argument. The stability of industry in the Western World is endangered by the current high energy costs and very possible energy shortages. As a result, the impoverishment of large sections of the population is to be feared. The consequences of this development are unpredictable. The 'earthlings' will have to come up with some new concepts – or the old wisdom like the Hermetic Principles – to meet this emergency.

Now I'll tell you what security layers of the Blue Planet I have to thwart in order to get to the Milky Way, and then to our Star Omicron 007.

The troposphere extends from the Blue Planet's crust to an altitude of about twelve kilometers. This relatively narrow layer contains all the air and oxygen that humans and animals need to breathe, as well as plants for photosynthesis. In this sphere, the temperature decreases with altitude because the only source of heat is the Earth's surface. This is also the densest layer because it bears the weight of the entire atmosphere above.

The weather of the Blue Planet builds up here. All clouds form here except for storm clouds, which reach up to the lowest layer of the stratosphere. Most air traffic takes place here, or in the transition region to the next shift.

The stratosphere is between twelve and fifty kilometers above the Earth's surface. This is the ozone layer that protects the Blue Planet from the Sun's harmful ultra-violet rays. These also cause the temperature to increase with altitude. It is the highest part of the atmosphere that airplanes can reach.

The mesosphere lies between fifty and sixty-five kilometers above the Blue Planet and gets colder with altitude. The top layer reaches the coldest temperature in the Earth's system, averaging minus eighty degree Celsius. Most of the meteors burn up there. However, rockets and rocket-propelled aircrafts can reach this layer.

The thermosphere is sixty-five to seven hundred kilometers above the Blue Planet. In this layer, the temperature increases with altitude due to the low density of the molecules. This layer is cloud- and water vapor free. The aurora borealis and the aurora australis can sometimes be seen here.

The exosphere lies between seven hundred and ten thousand kilometers above the Earth's crust. This is the highest layer of the Earth's atmosphere, which then combines with solar winds. Molecules have such a low density here that this layer does not behave like gas, and particles fly into space. Most of the Blue Planet's satellites orbit in this sphere.

The absolute boundary of the Blue Planet is difficult to define, because there is no clear line between the Blue Planet's atmospheres and space. And there my free ride begins, and I can write my 'Back to Galaxy' report. There seems to be just one possible danger – black holes with their incredibly high gravitational pull. But I have that under control.

Now for your sarcastic remarks about Marta. Not only did you do a great job of translating her emotional articles, but you improved them significantly with just a few changes. The duckling Marta understood and admired that. Basically, she was trying to flirt with you, not with me.

In addition, she found me to be quite old, she put me in my mid-thirties. Imagine her surprise if she found out about the big celebration of my one thousandth birthday! She would have fallen flat on her butt. We Star-dwellers don't have to die in order to develop further through reincarnations.

What should I do with this young duckling whose life form is based on carbon. Our building blocks are silicon in intricate compounds with other elements, including carbon. Silicon is one of the most abundant elements in the universe and so also on the Blue Planet. This element makes up 30% of the Earth's crust and is one hundred fifty times more abundant than carbon.

For chemists of the Blue Planet, no life form is possible on the basis of silicon, that supposedly only exists in Sci-Fi, like in Star Trek. This reminds me of the story of the bumblebee, which according to aerodynamic laws cannot fly, and yet it flies, unconcerned of the laws!

Just as the inhabitants of the Blue Planet still have elements of the ape in their DNA, there are also elements of 'homo sapiens' in us. I forgive your jealousy, I'm even proud of it. And it makes you even more lovable.

Of course the duckling Marta tried to flirt with me. It just goes to show that she's gotten over that 'narcissistic fling'. When – after her big look – I pointed to my ring, which you offered me for my birthday, she said with a little grimace: "That's how Bruce Willis reacted when a stewardess made eyes at him. But only in the cinema. By the way, tomorrow is another day!"

In a few years, Marta will have accumulated husband, children, dog and cat, as well as a few awards for her publications. As a present, I put my 'galaxophone' on her place in the library, covered with a sheet of paper on which a daffodil – the flower Narzisse – is blooming. She will understand.

Of course, I took out a special galactic chip. I know your mantra: "Trust is good, control is better." And I will place this chip in your beautiful hands.

I play no role in Marta's life. And that's good and right. Marta will only have to learn that on the Blue Planet she has to put up with caterpillars in order to meet butterflies.

And now my present for you: When Narcissus drowned, a daffodil bloomed at the edge of the spring, a flower symbolizing life. And I'll bring you a daffodil with roots and leaves from the Blue Planet!

As the duckling Marta correctly translated: 'The die is not cast', but rather: 'The dices are thrown up'. 'Narcissus' flower opposes narcissism. And this flower has great chances of overcoming all difficulties.

Gowinda, I'm coming home to the Stars. Don't wash you anymore!Who else, but Lotus!

Final alpha-mail to Star Omicron 007
Sent and received with joy!

THE END

General note

Much of the information was provided by the author's memory. Quotations from literature, biographical data regarding the protagonists, etc. were supplemented and checked from the Internet.

The author

Dr. mult. Traute Wohlers-Scharf studied law and political science, and later classical archeology at the University of Vienna. Then she started a career in international organizations such as IDEP (Dakar), UNIDO (Vienna), Asian Development Bank (Manila) and OECD (Paris). She stopped working internationally when her husband became ill. Then she completed professional training as a psychotherapist (symbolic drama) and worked as such in Vienna. Her interests include reading, playing bridge, golf, painting and pottery, as well as traveling and, more recently, healthy cooking. Her publications include the works "Forschungsgeschichte von Ephesos" (Peter Lang Verlag), "Tarot – Der Weg nach Innen" (Rainbow Spirit Verlag), "Trilateral Cooperation" (OECD, Paris), "Dictionary of Development Economics" (Elsevier Verlag) and "Eine Glücksfibel – / A Manual for Happiness – Vademecum for Eleonora und Tudora" (novum Verlag).

The publisher

> He who stops
> getting better
> stops being good.

This is the motto of novum publishing, and our focus
is on finding new manuscripts, publishing them and
offering long-term support to the authors.
Our publishing house was founded in 1997, and since
then it has become THE expert for new authors and
has won numerous awards.

**Our editorial team will peruse each manuscript
within a few weeks free of charge and without
obligation.**

You will find more information about
novum publishing and our books on the internet:

w w w . n o v u m p u b l i s h i n g . c o m